PUPPY PATROL ™

THE PUPPY PROJECT

D0974797

BOOKS IN THE PUPPY PATROL™ SERIES

COMING SOON

PUPPY PATROL ™

THE PUPPY PROJECT

JENNY DALE

Illustrations by Mick Reid

Cover illustration by Michael Rowe

AN
APPLE
PAPERBACK

SCHOLASTIC INC.

New York Toronto London Auckland Sydney
Mexico City New Delhi Hong Kong Buenos Aires

SPECIAL THANKS TO MARGARET McALLISTER

No part of this publication may be reproduced in whole or in part, or stored in a retrieval system, or transmitted in any form or by any means, electronic, mechanical, photocopying, recording, or otherwise, without written permission of the publisher. For information regarding permission, write to Macmillan Publishers Ltd., 25 Eccleston Place, London SW1W 9NF and Basingstoke.

ISBN 0-439-37968-7

Text copyright © 2002 by Working Partners Limited.
Illustrations copyright © 2002 by Mick Reid.

All rights reserved. Published by Scholastic Inc., 557 Broadway, New York, NY 10012 by arrangement with Macmillan Children's Books, a division of Macmillan Publishers Ltd.

SCHOLASTIC and associated logos are trademarks and/or registered trademarks of Scholastic Inc.

12 11 10 9 8 7 6 5 4 3 2 1   2 3 4 5 6 7/0

Printed in the U.S.A.   40
First Scholastic printing, December 2002

CHAPTER ONE

"**S**tay, Jake! Stay! Neil, hurry up! Jake won't sit still!"

"Hang on! I'm doing my best!" Eleven-year-old Neil Parker — the proud owner of a new camera — crouched down and pressed the shutter button. His sister, Emily, laughed and shook her brown hair from her eyes as she held the wriggling puppy in her arms. Jake was a young Border collie, full of energy. Not long ago he had been soft and chubby, but he was taller now, and his black-and-white coat grew thicker every week.

"He wants to go to you, Neil! I think he wants to play with the camera! You're not taking another one, are you?" protested Emily.

"I'm trying!" cried Neil as he attempted to keep Jake in the frame.

It was a chilly Sunday afternoon in the exercise field at King Street Kennels, near the small country town of Compton. Emily cuddled Jake close to her chest, but when Bob Parker strode into the field with Jake's father, Sam, at his heels, the pup squirmed free and scampered over to meet them.

"I brought Sam," called Bob. "I thought you'd want some pictures of him, too."

Neil ran up to the two Border collies as little Jake squared up to Sam, pressing his head down between his front paws and making a noise that was meant to be a growl.

"Sam doesn't want to play," Neil said to Jake as he bent down to pat the older dog. "You'll wear him out."

Dogs were the most important thing in Neil's life. His parents, Bob and Carole, ran a boarding kennel and rescue center at King Street as well as holding obedience classes. He loved all dogs, but Sam was his own dog and his greatest friend. Sam looked in top condition and still loved a good run around the field, but he had a heart condition, which meant that his life was constantly at risk. That was why Neil had spent some of his savings on a new camera. This way he could be sure of having plenty of pictures of Sam to keep, and of Jake, too.

"Sit, Sam!" ordered Neil. Sam, who was perfectly

trained, sat. "Jake, leave him alone." He took a picture just as Sam looked quizzically down at Jake as if the camera were some strange new toy Neil had just brought home. At the click of the shutter, Jake bounded up to Neil.

"Down, you silly thing! I've nearly finished the roll of film." He threw a stick for Jake and looked up at Emily. "I'm going to Mr. Hamley's now, to take photos of Dotty's pups. Are you coming?"

"Try and stop me!" said his sister, grinning. "And if Jake won't keep still, what will Dotty's puppies be like?"

Mr. Hamley was Neil and Emily's principal at Meadowbank School. His famously naughty Dalmatian, Dotty, had given birth to eight beautiful puppies a couple of months before. Neil had helped at their birth, which made them very special to him. Five had already gone to their new owners, but three lively, lovable pups were still with their mom.

Bob looked concerned. "Why do you want to go over there?" he asked. "Now that Mr. Hamley's the principal, he'll have a lot of extra work. He'll be busy enough without you two showing up."

"It's OK." Neil whistled for the dogs and began walking back to the house. "Smiler — I mean, Mr. Hamley — said I could come by anytime this weekend, and this is the last chance. The pups are going to their new home tomorrow."

"Rachel Hamley will be relieved," said Bob with a chuckle. "They've got enough on their hands with the new baby to look after."

Looking after their new baby, Martin, and the wildly energetic Dotty had been hard work for the Hamleys. So why had they decided to breed Dotty? Neil thought people were much harder to understand than dogs.

"At least it's down to three now," said Neil. "Someone came from the Lake District for one, two are with a dog-loving family near Manchester, and the other two have moved to a stately home in Northumberland. There are just two females left and one male, and he's the smallest. They call him Scrap."

"Won't Dotty miss her babies when they've all gone?" asked Emily wistfully.

"Mr. Hamley says she's had enough of their teasing," said Neil. "They pull her ears and chase her tail and never let her sleep. Oh, look, isn't that Kate?"

"It can't be," Emily said, puzzled. "It's Sunday — her day off."

They caught sight of a tall, blond figure as they got closer to the rescue center. Kate was the King Street kennel assistant.

"She's doing so much overtime just now, she may as well move in," said Bob as he waved to Kate. There was more work than ever at King Street. The Parkers had just opened a newer, larger rescue center with a walk-in dog clinic for local pets.

Kate came to meet them. Jake jumped up at her, and the rescue dogs, hearing voices, started barking loudly.

"Down, Jake!" she commanded and bent rather stiffly to pet him. She rubbed her back as she straightened up.

"Cleaning all those pens has done me in," she said. "I've finished here now. I'm going home for a steaming hot bath with half a ton of bubbles in it."

"You look exhausted," said Emily.

"Don't worry — help is at hand," Bob assured her. "We start interviewing for another assistant tomor-

row. You'll soon have someone else to work with. It'll
be good for you to have company."

"I've got lots of company," said Kate, nodding
toward the pens full of dogs. She walked with Neil
and Emily to the shed where the bikes were kept,
and they rode off together toward Compton.

Neil decided too late that ringing the doorbell at Mr.
Hamley's house wasn't a good idea. Dotty's loud,
keen barking was soon joined by excited little yaps
and then, rising louder and higher, the wailing of a
baby. A door banged somewhere, steps sounded in
the hall, and Mr. Hamley opened the door.

He didn't look at all the way he did at school. He
was bleary-eyed, his hair was a mess, his rumpled
sweater was covered in dog hair, and he wasn't
pleased to see them. He started to say something but
was interrupted by Dotty bounding past him and
nearly knocking everyone over. At Neil's command,
she remembered her manners and contented herself
with a noisy, licking, tail-wagging welcome.

Dotty was a mother now, but Neil wondered if she
would ever grow up. She was a beautiful dog, elegant
and well-balanced with dark, glossy spots. And, with
her overflowing energy, she was the most uncontrol-
lable dog Neil had ever met.

"You said we could take photos of the puppies,"
said Emily gently.

"Oh, yes. I suppose I did. You'd better come in." Mr.

Hamley led them to the kitchen. Rachel Hamley marched past with a brief nod of welcome, carrying the screaming baby Martin in one arm and a pile of clean laundry in the other. In the kitchen, everything seemed to be covered with a thin layer of white dog hair, the washing machine rumbled, and piles of damp baby clothes sat next to a box of dog food.

The Hamleys had made a roomy pen for the puppies against the wall. There were blankets, water dishes, and some very well-chewed toys.

Putting their soft paws against the mesh, two chubby, floppy, bright-eyed Dalmatian puppies wagged their short tails in delight. They pawed eagerly at the pen, pushing little black noses against Neil's and Emily's hands.

"You beauties!" cried Emily. "Aren't you growing fast!" She looked around at Mr. Hamley. "But shouldn't there be three?"

"Beauty's gone off exploring again," he said wearily. "The little one's Scrap, the bigger one's Berry. They've all figured out how to get out of there. No matter what we do to keep them in, they find a way around it, especially Beauty. She won't stay put for five minutes. She goes off and hides in corners. I've given up even trying with her."

Neil was about to laugh, but he could see that Mr. Hamley didn't find it funny. It was impossible not to laugh at Scrap, though, who was trying to chew his finger.

"No, Scrap," he said firmly. "You'll have to learn not to do that now your teeth are getting sharp."

"Can I pick them up?" asked Emily, who had already lost her heart to them.

"Yes, you may as well get them out before they manage it for themselves," said Mr. Hamley with a shrug. "You can take them into the garden for your photographs if you like."

Neil gathered a squirming bundle of puppy in his arms and glanced at his watch. "We won't be long," he said.

"Oh, take as long as you like," said Mr. Hamley, sounding irritated. "You could always come back tomorrow, or the next day, or the day after that."

"What do you mean?" asked Emily, looking puzzled. "They're going to new homes tomorrow, aren't they?"

Mr. Hamley rolled his eyes. "Not anymore. The buyers have changed their minds. They don't want them."

"Don't want them!" repeated Neil, who could hardly believe it.

Emily, stroking Berry's smooth, warm head, looked up in amazement. "Don't want them? How could anyone not want them?" She looked down into the deep, dark eyes of the puppy trying to lick her face. "How could anyone not want you, Berry?"

"You might think they're beautiful, Emily, but the buyers — they're a family called Arkwright — they wanted show dogs. Beauty and Berry looked all right to me, but now that their spots are beginning to develop, they're not quite right for the show circuit." He took Berry and ran a hand over her soft, spotted coat. "These spots are a bit patchy, really. Beauty's are the same, wherever she is. Show judges like perfectly round spots."

"I don't know why they need to be so fussy," said Neil. "And Scrap's spots are perfect."

"Yes, but he's small." Mr. Hamley sighed. "We were hoping he'd catch up with the others, but he hasn't. He'll always be on the petite side. Nobody will want him as a show dog. . . . Rachel's furious. She'd really counted on having the kitchen back to normal tomorrow. Goodness knows when we'll sell them now. Do you know of anyone who'd like Dalmatian pups, Neil?"

"I was about to say," said Neil, "I can put their details on our web site, if you like. That way, we can advertise them all over the country."

Neil turned his attention to Dotty as she dropped a blue rubber bone at his feet and sat back, her tail wagging hopefully. Neil threw the toy and watched the flailing jumble of legs as she raced after it. He wondered if she was jealous of all the attention the puppies were getting.

"Is she putting on weight, do you think?" he said.

"Could be," said Mr. Hamley. "She doesn't get as much exercise as she did, I'm afraid. There isn't time for long walks anymore."

"I'll take her now, if you like," said Neil. "Will you look after my camera, please? Don't let the puppies get near it!"

"I'll stay here and play with them," said Emily. She pressed her face against Berry's warm flank, then put her on the floor to play.

"I hope they can stay together," Emily continued. She looked around and then frowned. "Where's Beauty?"

"I suppose I'd better go and find her." Mr. Hamley sighed.

He left just in time, because Berry had been sniffing his shoelace and was about to chew it. Neil, clipping on Dotty's leash, turned around to find that Scrap had followed him and was now sitting at his heels, head to one side. Neil bent to stroke the silky ears.

"Sorry, Scrap," he said, "you're not old enough for long walks yet. Stay with Emily."

"He'll follow anyone around," replied Mr. Hamley from the sitting room. "He's always trotting after me and Rachel."

"That's sweet," said Emily.

"It's a nuisance," called Mr. Hamley. Soon he came back in, looking in cupboards and under the furniture as he searched for Beauty. "Rachel nearly broke her neck tripping over Scrap yesterday. We can't go on like this — I'm almost ready to *give* them away. Beauty, where are you?"

"I'll give Dotty her long walk," said Neil as Dotty jumped up to remind him that it was time to go. "I'll try and wear her out, if she —"

A cry of exasperation cut him short. Mrs. Hamley's voice rang down the stairs.

"Paul! I've found Beauty. She's behind the dressing table. And she's taken Martin's crib blankets in there! They'll have to be washed again! It's just too much!"

"Neil, I think I'll come with you after all," said Emily quickly, deciding they'd both better get out of the way. They took Dotty and made a fast escape. Finding homes for these puppies was suddenly number one on their priority list!

CHAPTER TWO

By the time Neil and Emily got back to King Street it was dark, but the lights were on at the rescue center. They could see a car parked outside.

"That's Dr. Harvey's car," said Emily. The doctor was an old friend of the family, and his two dogs had both been trained in Bob's obedience classes. There was Finn, a prizewinning Kerry blue, and a good-natured mongrel named Sandy.

The rescue center looked bright and welcoming inside and still had a shiny new appearance and a faint smell of fresh paint. Dr. Harvey, with his shaggy red beard and his old tweed jacket, sat in the waiting area. Smiling, he stood up to meet them. In his arms he held a small shaggy-coated mongrel with pointed ears like a fox. He chuckled as Neil and

Emily ran straight to the dog. It shivered a little and sniffed curiously at their hands before lifting up one ear and wagging its tail.

"Who's this?" said Neil.

"Goodness knows," said the doctor. "He's a stray. He was in the middle of the road — I nearly hit him."

"You've had a lucky escape, little mutt!" said Emily. "Are Mom and Dad around?"

"Bob's interviewing a candidate for the kennel assistant's job, I believe," said Dr. Harvey, scratching the little dog under the chin. One of his ears twitched forward. "When I went by the house, your mom told me that some young guy had turned up for his interview today instead of tomorrow. Carole was just on her way out, so I'm waiting to introduce Bob to this little stray — at least, I think he must be a stray."

He smiled warmly down at the dog, who craned his neck to look up at him. He gave a trustful wag of the tail and another twitch of the ear, and Neil scratched the top of his head. The dog twisted around to lick Neil's wrist.

"Silly thing, running into the road like that," said Emily gently. "You could have been killed."

"That's what I told him," agreed Dr. Harvey. "I did a perfect emergency stop and got out to see if he had a name tag. The minute the car door opened, he jumped up and sat in the passenger seat, asking for a ride! Anyway, he's not wearing a collar, so I brought him to the brand-new five-star rescue center."

Dr. Harvey sat down and put the dog on the floor at his feet. Neil ran his hands over the mongrel and reached into his pocket for a dog treat, which the little dog gobbled down immediately.

"I gave him some water and a couple of dog biscuits that I had in the car," said Dr. Harvey. "They vanished like snow in summer! I wonder how long he's been on the run?"

"Probably not long," said Neil. "He's a bit on the thin side, but not starving. And he's young. He still has a bit of puppyishness about him." The dog lay down, put his head on one side, twitched both ears, and stared hard at Neil's pocket.

"Just one more, then," said Neil. "I shouldn't give you too much at once." As the dog crunched up the treat and put his paws on Neil's knee for attention, Neil warmed to the trusting little stray, whose ears were twitching more than ever.

"He has very expressive ears, whoever he is," remarked Dr. Harvey. "I wish I could do that."

Outside, a door opened and Bob appeared from the kennel office with a young man. Neil and Emily glanced at each other and tried not to stare. It was his hair they noticed first — it was pink and green and sculpted into spikes. He wore a long jacket dotted with badges, purple-and-yellow patchwork trousers, and purple-painted boots. Bob showed him out and came back shaking his head.

"Is that your new fashion expert, Bob?" Dr. Harvey asked with a grin.

"No, and he's not our new kennel assistant, either," said Bob. He looked at Neil and Emily. "And you two can stop giggling. He looks strange, but his heart's in the right place. He cares a lot about animals, and he's got a brain in there. Too bad he doesn't know which day of the week it is."

"You mean he didn't realize it was Sunday?" asked Emily.

Bob nodded.

"What was he like with the dogs?" asked Neil.

"Oh, no problems there. He likes them, he knows how to handle them and talk to them, and they liked him. But he comes across as completely disorganized. His fashion sense might put some of our customers off, too, unfortunately. The owners, not the dogs," he added, and Neil and Emily giggled again. "Dogs have more sense than people. They don't judge by appearances. Now, Alex, where did this mutt come from?"

Alex Harvey explained about the dog as Bob, talking kindly to the animal, looked at his coat and paws. The dog's ears drooped as Bob inspected his teeth, but otherwise he put up with it all patiently.

"He might be an unwanted Christmas present," said Neil.

"Mmm — I'm not so sure. It's a bit late for that. We'll put him in the rescue block." Bob patted the dog's head. "I don't think he's been ill-kept. He didn't growl when I checked him over."

"Listen! Mom's coming home," said Emily as the familiar sound of the Range Rover's engine grew louder as it slowed to a stop on the gravel in the driveway outside. The dog stopped sniffing Bob's hands. He sat up straight. His ears twitched one at a time, then both together, and he turned his head to the sound.

Neil and Emily hurried to the door, nearly falling over the dog as he tore past them. Carole opened the car door and jumped out, and there was a burst of sudden delighted laughter.

Five-year-old Sarah, ribbons falling out of her hair and cake crumbs around her mouth, already had the dog in her arms. "Hello!" She giggled. "You're friendly!"

The dog wriggled free from her. He scrambled into the driver's seat, put both front paws on the steering wheel, and looked from side to side.

"I think he likes cars!" said Neil. "We should call him Wheelie. Or Damon, after . . ."

"Wheelie will do," said Bob firmly. "I'm not shouting 'Damon' down the exercise field. We'll write up a description of him and try to find out if anyone's looking for him. When Mike comes in for the next clinic, he can check to see if he's got a microchip implant. He may even recognize him if he's local." Mike Turner was the Parkers' vet. He had a veterinary practice in Compton and now regularly held dedicated canine clinics at King Street. "Leave him with me, Alex," added Bob as he took the little dog in his arms.

The doctor was looking intently at the top of Bob's head.

"What's so interesting?" asked Bob.

"I was imagining pink and green spikes," said Dr. Harvey. "And the beard tinted to match. You should try it. It should be a nice subject for Neil's camera."

"It would break the lens," said Neil.

"And," said Dr. Harvey, with a tug at Neil's short brown hair that already stuck out in all directions, "what do you think for your brother, Emily? An apricot poodle cut?"

When Wheelie had been settled into the rescue center and the family had finished dinner, Neil and Emily explained to their parents about Dotty's puppies and their sudden need for new homes. Jake was stretched out asleep in front of the fire, and Sam lay serenely at Neil's feet.

"The sooner they can get those puppies out of there, the better," agreed Bob. "They'll get livelier every day, and they'll get into more and more mischief as well. Yes, of course you can put the details on the web site, if that's what Mr. Hamley wants."

"Mrs. Hamley's going out of her mind about them," said Neil. "They just seem to have taken over, and she can't wait to get everything back to normal."

"Somebody's bound to want them soon," said Emily. "They're such lovely puppies."

"I wish I could see them," said Sarah.

"Unfortunately," said Carole sadly, "the world is full of lovely puppies. And there aren't enough good homes for them. I wish we didn't need any rescue centers at all." She smiled down at Sarah, who was playing with Fudge, her pet hamster.

"Fudge has forgotten all of his ballet steps," said

Sarah as Fudge ran up her arm. "I'll have to teach him again. Can you get black-and-white-spotted hamsters, like Dalmatians?"

Neil laughed.

"I don't think so, dear," said Carole. "If there is such a thing as a Dalmatian hamster, I'm sure it wouldn't be as nice as Fudge!" She glanced at Neil, and Sarah beamed with pride.

"I sometimes think Sarah's got the right idea, keeping a hamster," said Carole. "Small pets are a lot less trouble. If Paul's willing to let us help, we'll do what we can for Dotty's litter. Three puppies, a baby, and Dotty! Poor Paul and Rachel must be going out of their minds. How on earth do they cope?"

"By the look of things," said Emily as she stroked Jake's ears, "they don't."

"They're desperate," said Neil, "and that worries me. If we don't help them find good homes for the puppies soon, they might sell to anybody, without checking to be sure they'd be good owners."

When the school bell rang the next morning, Neil made his way to Mr. Hamley's office. His friends Chris and Hasheem called down the corridor after him.

"Neil! Where are you going? You'll be late for roll call!" shouted Hasheem.

"I need to see Smiler, about finding new homes for Dotty's pups. If I'm late, Hasheem, can you explain to . . . um . . ." Now that Mr. Hamley had been made principal, Neil was never quite sure who would be taking his class from one day to the next.

"Our new teacher starts today," said Hasheem. "Yes, I'll tell him — or her. See you later!"

"Hasheem!" Neil had just thought of something else. "Tell the teacher why I need to see Mr. Hamley, will you? Otherwise it might look like I'm in trouble."

"Or in the doghouse!" Chris laughed.

Chris and Hasheem suddenly stopped laughing and walked quietly to their classrooms, so Neil knew they must have caught sight of Mr. Hamley. He was on his way down the corridor, looking much neater than he had the day before, but his eyes still had dark shadows under them. He motioned to Neil to follow him into the study, where he heaved his briefcase onto the desk and brushed a few white dog hairs from his sleeve.

"Yes, Neil, what is it?"

"I talked to my dad last night about the puppies. We'll put their descriptions on our web site, if that's OK with you. We should get lots of interest. People from all over the country contact us about dogs."

"That's very helpful of you, Neil," said Mr. Hamley. "The sooner the puppies are gone, the better." He sat down behind his desk and sighed. "I don't think it was such a good idea breeding Dotty when we did, you know. I had no idea how much work it would be — all that feeding and cleaning up. And now they want to explore all the time. They think everything's a toy."

"All dogs do that," said Neil. "They're just like little kids."

"Little kids don't eat the tablecloth," said Mr. Hamley. "Berry did."

Neil smothered a laugh. "I didn't think Berry was too bad," he said. "All dogs chew things."

"Well, she's taken to scratching doors now if she can't get to wherever Beauty is. The kitchen door looks terrible. Rachel can't turn her back for a minute without some small disaster happening. And Martin . . ." He looked at his watch. "Never mind all this, Neil. You should be in your classroom. Off you go. And don't run in the hall."

Neil was at the classroom door before he remembered that he didn't know who his new teacher was. Perhaps he should keep his fingers crossed. Hoping for the best and fearing the worst, he opened the door.

CHAPTER THREE

A small woman with neat blond hair was sitting at the teacher's desk in Neil's classroom. She wore a dark suit and glasses and looked up sternly as Neil came in.

"Neil Parker, I presume? Come here, please." Neil stood at her desk. "I'm your new teacher, Mrs. Sharpe. I understand you've been to see Mr. Hamley?"

"Yes, Mrs. Sharpe."

"This wasn't on school business, was it?"

"Not exactly, but —"

"Then you shouldn't have used lesson time. Couldn't it have waited until break? Now, if you look at the board you'll see the history exercise I've just given the rest of the class. Settle down quickly, please, Neil. Don't forget: neatness and accuracy."

Neil felt as if he should salute. He hurried to his place, sorted out his books, and rushed to scribble down the work on the board.

"Sharpe, as in razor sharp," whispered Hasheem. "She must have trained in the army."

"Hasheem Lindon, that's enough," said Mrs. Sharpe without even looking up. But Neil, looking up from his work, saw a smile twitching at the corners of her mouth.

Mrs. Sharpe kept the class hard at work all day. Even Mr. Hamley had never been so demanding. As everyone was leaving, she called Neil to her desk.

"Neil, I need to check your address," she said. "I'm not sure if there's a mistake in this register. It says 'King Street Kennels' here. You're not a dog, are you?"

Neil grinned and explained about the Puppy Patrol. She listened with interest and smiled. "I like dogs, but they can be a lot of trouble," she said. "I was talking on the phone last night to my next-door neighbor from Jedburgh, where I used to live — I've just moved down here from Scotland. Her dog's missing, and she's frantic with worry. . . . Now, will you take this folder to Mr. Hamley, please? We've got a staff meeting soon, and he'll need to read it before we start."

Neil met Emily in the hall, and they went together to give Mr. Hamley the folder.

"This ridiculous meeting," grumbled Mr. Hamley. He looked as if he'd like to drop the folder in the trash can. "It would have to be tonight. Rachel's already had all the dogs and Martin to deal with since I went out this morning. It's not fair to her if I'm home late again."

"Can we go and help?" said Emily. "We could feed the puppies and keep them out of her way."

"And I could take Dotty for another long walk," said Neil hopefully. "It would get her out from under Mrs. Hamley's feet."

"That would be a big help," said Mr. Hamley. He looked relieved. "She's at her wits' end. I'll phone your parents now and let them know where you're going. And I'll call Rachel to say you're coming. Thanks. I'll get home as soon as I can."

"I wish I had my gloves with me," said Emily, stuffing her hands deep into her pockets as they walked to the Hamleys' house. "It's freezing."

They could see their breath forming chilly clouds in front of them. By the time they reached the house, Neil's ears and toes were tingling with cold.

Nobody came to the door when they rang the bell, but, as usual, they heard Dotty's noisy barking. It sounded even louder than usual — and closer.

"It sounds like she's *outside*," said Neil. "Listen!"

There was another series of barks and the sound of paws scrabbling against the backyard gate. Puppy voices yapped and whimpered urgently as Neil and Emily ran to investigate. It was a solid wooden gate, too high for even Dotty to jump, and with no room underneath for a small puppy to squeeze through. Dotty's head and paws popped up, and a row of three inquisitive little black noses appeared under the gate, sniffing eagerly from side to side.

"That's where you are!" said Neil. "Look out for the puppies, Em, don't let them run off." He opened the gate just enough to squeeze through so Dotty couldn't run out. Once they were in, Emily held on to the puppies and herded them away from the gate until it was safely shut again.

"It's much too cold for them to be out," said Neil. "Mrs. Hamley should be with them. Do you think she's gone out?"

"Scrap's freezing!" gasped Emily. "You come here, Scrap, and get warm." She picked up the shivering pup and cuddled him as he nestled against her for comfort. "I wonder how long they've been out here? Feel him, Neil, he's really cold!"

While Scrap huddled against Emily's shoulder, Beauty and Berry scampered to the back doorstep, desperate to get back into the warm kitchen. They, too, were shivering as they huddled together, and Beauty whined softly. Berry pawed at the door, lost her balance, tumbled off the step, and clambered back to cuddle up to her sister.

"Come here, you two," said Neil. He picked up one in each arm, and they pressed against him for warmth. "At least Dotty's got a full-grown adult coat, but this isn't doing the puppies any good!"

"What's going on?" Emily peeked in at a window, trying to see any sign of life in the house. "Where's Mrs. Hamley?"

"I hope she turns up soon," said Neil, shivering, "before we all freeze to death!"

As he spoke, the back door opened and Mrs. Hamley appeared. She looked cross and flustered, and her hair was straggled as if it hadn't been brushed all day. On her hip she carried baby Martin, who was rubbing his eyes and looked very pink in the cheeks. Neil and Emily set the puppies down on the doorstep and the three eager little Dalmatians scampered into the house, followed by Dotty.

Mrs. Hamley looked past them at Neil and Emily. "Hello, you two. Paul just phoned to say you were coming. You could have come right in. I wouldn't have minded." She put her free hand to her mouth to stifle a yawn. "I was too tied up to come to the door."

Neil and Emily exchanged anxious glances.

Inside, the kitchen looked worse than ever. The dogs' bowls sat unwashed outside their pen. A pile of clean diapers had been knocked off a chair and it looked as if the puppies had been making a nest in them. Pieces of half-eaten dog biscuits were scattered on the floor between two newspapers that were wet and dark in the middle. This, and the mop and bucket propped against the wall, told Neil that Mrs. Hamley must have been trying to clean up puppy puddles when she put the dogs outside. She clearly had wanted to avoid any more puddles. The room smelled of puppies and disinfectant.

"Beauty!" snapped Mrs. Hamley. Beauty had returned to the nest of diapers. She stopped burrowing and looked up innocently, with a clean white diaper half over her head and half in her mouth. Neil quickly picked her up and took it away before she could do any more damage. Emily, smiling, put out a hand toward the curly-haired baby. Mrs. Hamley gently drew Martin away.

"Not when you've been handling the puppies, Emily. You can hold Martin after you've washed your hands. Put them all in the pen, please, Neil, and they might sleep for ten minutes. I wish *I* could."

"It's better if we hold on to them, Mrs. Hamley," said Neil. Emily took Berry and Scrap in her arms, though Scrap struggled free and padded to Mrs. Hamley's feet. "They're cold — much colder than they should be. How long were they out?"

Neil couldn't help saying it. He always thought of dogs first and everything else afterward. But he could see from Mrs. Hamley's face that his remark had not gone over well. She tightened her lips as if she needed all her self-control not to scream. She wiped drool from Martin's chin with a tissue. Then she turned to Neil, and the anger she was controlling blazed from her eyes.

"Neil," she said, "it wasn't my idea to have Dotty bred to end up with a house full of puppies that we can't sell. Dogs may be the whole world for you, but the most important thing for me is Martin, and he takes a lot of looking after. I haven't had a decent night's sleep since he was born."

She seemed close to crying. Neil held Beauty close and looked awkwardly at the floor.

"I just hope Martin hasn't caught anything from them," she went on. "It's impossible to housebreak three at once when I've got Martin to look after as well, so I'm always cleaning up after them. Everything has to be clean for babies, so I keep washing and sterilizing his toys because the dogs have gotten ahold of them. And I tripped over Scrap this morning with Martin in my arms. He wasn't hurt, but I can't bear to think what might have happened!"

Scrap, hearing his name, looked up adoringly at her. She ruffled his ears kindly. "I'm fond of the puppies," she said, "but they're making my life impossible!"

She was trembling with rage and distress. Neil and Emily glanced at each other, unsure of what to do next.

"I'm sorry. We only wanted to help," said Neil.

"I'm sorry, too." She smiled weakly. "I do appreciate your being here."

"Well, we can clean up," said Emily, picking up a rubber bone and a tooth-marked ball. "And tell us where the cleaning stuff is, and we'll mop up the puddles. We're used to that."

"It would be a big help," said Mrs. Hamley. "Then I could give Martin his baby food. He's starving."

She washed her hands and put a bowl of something that looked like wallpaper paste into the microwave. Then, with the bowl, a bib, and Martin, she disappeared into the dining room. Scrap trotted after her, but Neil gently stopped him.

He soon found out what she meant about tripping

over Scrap. The puppy trotted devotedly after him, sitting down so close behind him that it was hard not to step on a paw by accident. Scrap couldn't quite decide who was his best friend, Neil or the mop. But, after having a good sniff at both and challenging the mop to a fight, he decided Neil smelled more interesting and sat down just where Neil would stumble over him as he turned around.

"Scrap, you silly thing!" Neil put him gently back in the pen and gave him a hug to reassure him that he wasn't in trouble. "Emily, where are the other two?"

Emily looked around. "They were there a moment ago. Oh, Neil, the door into the hall's open. They could be anywhere. Let's find them quickly."

Mrs. Hamley, spooning the baby food into a very messy Martin, hadn't seen the puppies, either. Neil and Emily tried cabinets and corners and looked behind chairs and under beds, but with no success. Finally, Emily pointed out that the only room they hadn't tried was the bathroom.

Two guilty little black-and-white faces peeked out at them from the shower. Beauty had pulled down a towel and still had one end in her teeth. It trailed wetly across the floor, and a few shreds of pink sponge stuck out of Berry's mouth. Beauty dropped her towel and made one last attempt to make a nest with the shower curtain.

"Wish I had the camera," said Neil. "Come on, you pair of monkeys. No, Berry, you can't have the rubber duck. Scrap! You're under my feet again!" Somehow, he had gotten out of the pen.

They carried Beauty and Berry downstairs, with Scrap following. Back in the kitchen, Dotty was wild with excitement for the exercise she needed so much. Neil treated her to a long walk, with a good run off the leash. By the time he came back, everything seemed strangely peaceful. The puppies were fast asleep, curled around one another in a warm huddle. Emily was taking a cup of tea in to Mrs. Hamley.

Rachel Hamley rocked a very sleepy Martin against her shoulder. "Thanks, Emily," she said. "I think I can put Martin in his crib now."

Then, Mr. Hamley came through the back door, briefcase in hand.

Dotty set off a volley of barking so loud it was painful. Martin, startled out of his nap, screamed. Three yapping puppy voices joined in.

"Oh, *Paul!*" cried Mrs. Hamley as the puppies, wide awake again, scrambled to meet him. The sudden excitement was too much for them. Almost at the same time, three puddles appeared on the floor. Neil, seeing Scrap positioning himself for something more than a puddle, grabbed him and rushed him outside.

"What's the matter with Berry?" called Mrs. Hamley. "Look at her!"

From the back door, Neil could see what was the matter with Berry. Her head was down, her mouth was open, and she was straining her neck. He ran for the nearest newspaper and pushed it in front of her just as she threw up the rest of the chewed pink sponge.

"That's better, good girl," Neil said, reassuring her. "It's all right, Mrs. Hamley. She got it all on the newspaper."

"It *isn't* all right," said Mrs. Hamley, her mouth tight. "That's today's paper. I hadn't read it." She looked very pale and trembled as if she was about to explode.

Mr. Hamley stood stock-still — his eyes riveted on his angry wife. He smelled trouble.

Neil and Emily got very quiet.

Even the dogs quit their antics and looked up at her.

Then Mrs. Hamley spoke. "I'm going to pack," she said quietly. "Martin and I are going to my parents' tonight, and we'll stay there until these puppies are gone for good. I can't stand one more day of this." And, as she stormed out of the room, not even Scrap dared to follow her.

CHAPTER FOUR

Neil and Emily were halfway home before either of them spoke.

"I never thought she'd do that," said Neil at last.

"Neither did Mr. Hamley," said Emily. "This is serious. We really have to get those puppies new homes."

They were soon at their own front gate, and through the kitchen window they could see Bob reaching for the oven mitts. That was a good sign. Carole was on her way across from the rescue center with a plump, pretty girl who waved cheerfully as she walked away. As Neil opened the front door, Jake and Sam raced to meet them, sniffing with curiosity.

"They want to know which dogs I've been with this time," said Neil, patting Jake with one hand and

Sam with the other. "You can smell Dotty, can't you, Sam?"

"I knew you'd turn up as soon as there was food on the table," called Bob. "It's ready now, so hurry and wash up."

They gathered around the table as Sarah announced that they were having worms for dinner. Carole quietly told her not to make rude remarks about the spaghetti.

Emily changed the subject. "Was that girl here for an interview?" she asked.

"She was, yes," said Carole. "She's kind and good-natured and very relaxed. But she seems too laid-back to me. We need somebody who'll keep up our high standards. We've worked hard to build up our reputation, and we can't risk losing it."

"Only the best for King Street," said Bob. "We'll see what the next one's like. How was everybody at the Hamley house?"

"How much time have you got?" said Neil.

Neil and Emily told them everything that had happened while Bob and Carole listened sympathetically. When she heard about Berry and the sponge, Carole couldn't drink her tea for laughing, but she grew grave and concerned when she heard the rest of the story.

"Well! This *is* serious," she said. "It's been hard on Rachel. I know she shouldn't have left the puppies outside, but she probably didn't realize how much colder it was getting. The Hamleys had no idea what they were getting themselves in to. Babies and puppies aren't a good mix."

"You managed it, Mom," said Neil.

"Mom can do anything!" said Sarah.

"I've been around animals all my life," replied Carole. "And we weren't running King Street when you were born, Neil."

"You were when Sarah was born," Emily pointed out.

"Yes, but I knew which way was up with a baby by then. And this is a well-established kennel business. We've got proper facilities and staff to make sure it runs smoothly. That's very different from one woman and a house full of puppies. Our dogs don't live in the house, except for Sam and His Lordship there." Jake looked up and beat his tail on the floor.

"Dotty's puppies are very naughty," admitted Emily. "Take Dotty, add energy, take away the little sense she's got, and multiply by three. Nothing's safe from them."

"Then I'm not surprised Rachel felt she had to get out," said Carole.

"But baby animals are sweet," said Sarah. "If Fudge met a lady hamster, they could have babies."

"Fudge wouldn't like that," said Carole quickly. "He wouldn't have all your attention to himself anymore, would he? Now, if you're all finished, you can clear the table."

When the table was cleared, Neil and Bob went to the rescue center. Neil was anxious to see how Wheelie was settling in. The little dog gave them a happy, ear-twitching greeting, and, as Neil opened the door of his pen, he brought a rubber ball and laid it hopefully at his feet.

"He's not pining, then," said Neil. He threw the ball, and Wheelie ran to pounce on it, carry it back, and drop it at his feet.

"He eats whatever I put in front of him, too," said Bob. "He's a friendly, trusting character and easily pleased. But he's a mystery. You thought he might be an abandoned Christmas puppy, didn't you, Neil?"

"Well, yes," he admitted. "But I'm not sure now."

"Mike saw him today. He figures he's about a year old," said Bob. "That's a little old for a Christmas puppy. He's in good condition, and there's no sign that he's ever been ill-treated. He trusts everyone."

Neil and Wheelie had a good game going by now. Neil hid the ball behind himself and showed the dog his empty hands, but it didn't take Wheelie long to find it.

"But," Bob went on, "no collar and no microchip — Mike scanned him. And no inquiries about him."

Neil slipped the ball under his jacket, where Wheelie sniffed it out and barked to have it thrown back. Neil threw it again. "He's been someone's friend, Dad. They must be missing him. I would, if he was my dog. I'll check the computer again, in case anybody's looking for him."

Neil checked the web site again that night. There were two inquiries about missing dogs, but neither of them answered Wheelie's description. Nobody had shown any interest in the Dalmatian puppies, either. Perhaps it was too soon. The need to find them owners was urgent, though, and would become more urgent every day that Rachel Hamley stayed away from home. When he had switched off the computer, Neil heard Carole talking to somebody over the phone.

"Yes, Paul, no problem," she was saying. "Bring them all in on your way to school in the morning. No, we don't usually take unvaccinated pups, but, since it's you, we'll make an exception. We'll keep them in a well-scrubbed pen, isolated from the other dogs. We'll see you in the morning."

"Mom," said Neil, "was that . . . ?"

"Mr. Hamley? Yes," she said. "Guess who's coming to stay! With Rachel away, there's nobody at home to look after Dotty and the puppies, so they're coming here as boarders. I'll phone Kate tonight. She's going to love this!"

Mr. Hamley arrived early the next morning, just as Kate was wheeling her bike to the shed. Neil and Emily ran outside to find her exclaiming with delight over the three puppies, who pawed happily at the car windows.

"Don't let them out yet, Mr. Hamley," she was saying. "They shouldn't be put on the ground where other dogs have been. Here, Neil, Emily, do you want to help me with them?"

Together, they carried the delighted puppies to their designated pen. Mr. Hamley had brought bedding and toys from home to help the dogs settle down in their new surroundings, and the three puppies were soon sniffing inquisitively into corners as they tumbled around the run. As Bob came to join them, Dotty put her paws on Mr. Hamley's shoulders for a farewell lick.

"I've checked the web site," said Neil. "No response

about the puppies yet, but we should get some interest soon."

"Don't worry about it," said Mr. Hamley, taking Neil by surprise. He was a great deal calmer than he'd been the previous evening, in the middle of the noise and puddles. "There's a couple, the Waverley-Bells, who want to see them tonight."

"Who?" said Neil.

"Charles and Pamela Waverley-Bell," said Mr. Hamley with a glance at Bob. "They breed and sell pedigree dogs. One of the teachers at school lives near them and knew I wanted homes for three puppies. When the Waverley-Bells heard about them, they seemed really excited. Can they come here to see the puppies, Bob? She sounded like a pleasant, sensible person when I spoke to her over the phone."

"No problem," said Bob. "I'd like to meet them. I haven't heard that name before."

"Come on, then, you two," Mr. Hamley said to Neil and Emily. "If you're ready in five minutes, I can give you a ride to school. By the way, are you keeping up with your homework? I hope all this dog-sitting doesn't keep you from it."

"Of course not!" insisted Neil. With Mrs. Sharpe in charge, nobody would ever dare neglect homework.

When Neil was leaving school that day, he found Toby Sparrow waiting outside the classroom. Toby's parents ran Pretty Paws. Pretty Paws was a sort of "dog hotel" where small pedigree dogs went to be pampered, shampooed, and treated like film stars.

"I might be coming over to King Street tonight," Toby said eagerly. "Emily told me about that stray dog that jumps into cars. Mom says she'll try and come by King Street later to have a look at him and see if she knows whose he is."

"Great!" said Neil. Relations between Pretty Paws and King Street seemed to be better now. It had been a struggle when the "doggy hotel" had first opened. Competition for King Street Kennels had made everyone feel uncomfortable. "You might be lucky and get to see Dotty's puppies," added Neil. "They're boarding with us at the moment."

"Dotty's puppies?" Toby's eyes brightened, and a wistful look crossed his face. "Haven't they all gone yet?"

Neil knew how much Toby wanted a puppy. Not long ago, he had helped to rescue three abandoned puppies and had been heartbroken when he wasn't allowed to keep one for himself. Even though the Sparrow family worked with dogs, Neil wasn't sure if Toby was ready for one of his own. He'd certainly give it love and kindness, but Neil knew that wasn't enough. He would need commitment, patience, and firmness, too.

"Dalmatians are boisterous dogs," said Neil. "Look at Dotty."

"Great!" said Toby.

Neil smiled. "The thing is," he went on, "they're hard to train. And they grow big and strong, so they're not easy to handle."

"I'd learn," Toby said eagerly, and his eyes were bright. "If I had one, I'd bring it to your dad's classes. We'd practice training every day. And I'd take it for plenty of walks."

"Even on cold mornings when it's pouring rain and you have to take the dog out before school?" said Neil, who often had mornings like this.

"I wouldn't mind that," said Toby. "Well, maybe I would, sometimes, but I'd do it, anyway. I help a lot with the Pretty Paws dogs. Neil, do you think there's any chance I could have one of Dotty's pups?"

"You'll have to ask your mom first," said Neil carefully. "And if she said yes, it would still be up to Mr. Hamley."

Even as he said this, Neil knew that Mr. Hamley was desperate enough to sell the pups to absolutely anyone. But that was the trouble.

Toby and his mother arrived at King Street in the evening, and Carole took Mrs. Sparrow to the rescue center to see Wheelie. Toby looked hopefully at Neil.

"You want to see the spotted gang, don't you?" said Neil. "Come on, then, I'll take you to the pen."

It was not long since the puppies had been fed, and they were curled in a sleepy heap of paws and ears and black button noses. Toby knelt in front of the mesh and gazed at them. Dotty, who was wide awake, bounded across, barking, to welcome them.

"Quiet! Good girl!" said Neil. "That's what they're like, Toby, when they grow up."

"Real big, doggy dogs," said Toby with longing. "Wow, Neil! Look at the pups!"

Neil looked. Disturbed by Dotty's barking, Beauty and Berry woke up halfway, stretched, yawned enormously, and went back to sleep. But Scrap had noticed the visitors and was padding across the floor to them, his eyes bright and his tail wagging hard.

"His name's Scrap," said Neil.

"Scrap!" called Toby. "Come on, Scrap!"

Toby put one hand on the mesh. Scrap sniffed at his fingers and took a lick.

"We'd better go," said Neil, suddenly feeling uneasy. Perhaps he shouldn't have brought Toby to see the puppies. It was love at first sight. If Toby could have Scrap, it would be one less puppy for Mr. Hamley to worry about and the fulfillment of Toby's dreams. But could Toby provide a good home for a growing dog? And would his mother allow him to have a puppy? If not, he would be heartbroken.

CHAPTER FIVE

"**A**re you still in there?" called Mrs. Sparrow. "Time to go, Toby."

Toby tore himself away from the dogs in the rescue center, still gazing over his shoulder on the way out.

"Mom . . ." he began, but his mother stopped him.

"I know what you're going to ask. And I'm not making any promises. We'll talk about it, that's all," she said firmly.

Neil and Carole watched them go.

"Did she recognize Wheelie?" asked Neil.

"No. Didn't have a clue about him," said Carole. "But she has much more dog sense since she's been taking the kennel-management course. If Toby did get a puppy, she'd make sure he took good care of it.

Hang on, who on earth is this?" she asked as a very shiny Range Rover swooshed into the drive.

"Someone with a brand-new car," said Neil. "And Mr. Hamley's in it!"

They could already see Bob on his way to greet the new arrivals. As Neil approached he could hear Mr. Hamley, who sounded pleased, introducing his new friends.

"Charles and Pamela Waverley-Bell," he said. "They're interested in buying the puppies."

The Waverley-Bells, smiling and friendly, were already shaking hands with Bob. Both were very well-spoken. They were about fifty, plainly but neatly dressed in tweed clothes. The man was tall and wore a cap and a rain jacket, and Mrs. Waverley-Bell was a squarely built woman with neatly styled graying hair and sensible shoes. Neil joined the group as they went with Mr. Hamley and Bob to the boarding kennels. Mr. Hamley looked very pleased with himself.

"You're new to this area, I think?" said Bob.

"Yes, we've just moved to one of the big houses on Riverside Road, just this side of Colshaw," said Mr. Waverley-Bell. "We needed a place with outbuildings we could convert into kennels."

"I've seen the kennels," said Mr. Hamley quickly. "They're very clean and comfortable."

"And what breeds do you deal in?" asked Bob, leading the way to Dotty's pen.

"Oh, a wide range," said Mr. Waverley-Bell. "Westies,

Chihuahuas, retrievers, and Dalmatians, of course. It's difficult to run a successful business by specializing in just one breed. We prefer to offer our clients a choice. Dalmatians are very popular just now."

They reached Dotty's pen, and Neil expected to see the usual smile of delight when anyone saw the puppies. Bob opened the door and, as Dotty hurled herself at Mr. Hamley, Neil watched the Waverley-Bells.

Without saying a word, they bent down and each picked up a puppy. With careful attention, Charles Waverley-Bell held Berry in one arm while he inspected her teeth and ran his free hand over the shape of her head. She took a playful lick at his wrist, but he ignored her.

"Mmmm," was all he said.

Pamela Waverley-Bell was examining Beauty's paws with great care. Neil picked up Scrap, who nestled in his arms, looking up at his face. For a pen full of puppies, it was strangely quiet.

Mr. Waverley-Bell spoke at last. "She has a very nice head," he said. "It's a pity about her markings. She's a strong pup, though."

His wife held Beauty at a distance to take a better look at her.

"Will this one be good enough to breed from? That's the question," she said. "I wonder how she'll turn out when she's fully grown. As you say, the markings are patchy. Hardly any spots on her tail, which is a shame." She balanced Beauty's tail in one hand, then passed the puppy to Mr. Hamley with a polite smile and took Scrap. In her large hands, he looked tinier than ever.

The way they handled the dogs baffled Neil. They may as well have been holding two suitcases or two bags of groceries. The Waverley-Bells weren't unkind or careless. They handled the puppies expertly, checking their bone structure and their markings. But neither of them spoke to the pups. They didn't bother to make friends with them or calm them. There was no stroking, no affection, no play. They didn't even smile. How could anyone hold Scrap and not smile?

Neil glanced up at Mr. Hamley and tried to catch his eye, but he was looking at Scrap in Pamela Waverley-Bell's efficient hands. Dotty stood beside him, unusually still and controlled, observing all that happened.

At last, the Waverley-Bells looked at each other, and both raised their eyebrows.

"We'll have to talk it over," said Mrs. Waverley-Bell. She put Scrap on the floor, and he immediately scampered to Neil's outstretched hands.

"I see," said Mr. Hamley. "Well, thanks, Bob. We'll get out of your way now."

Neil was still thinking of the bright, longing face of Toby Sparrow. He urgently needed a word with Mr. Hamley in private.

"Mr. Hamley, will you just have a quick look at my homework, please?" he said. "It's really important."

Mr. Hamley put Beauty on the floor and followed Neil outside.

"Is it really homework that's suddenly so important, Neil?" he asked.

"No, Mr. Hamley, but I had to talk to you privately," he said. "I don't like the look of them. They're not taking any real interest in the puppies."

"They look very interested to me."

"Yes, but they don't treat the pups as" — Neil nearly said *people* — "as *personalities*. They don't look as if they really *care*."

"You may see it like that, Neil. But to me, they just look like professionals."

"And there's something else," said Neil. "Toby

Sparrow was asking about the puppies today. He'd love one."

Mr. Hamley looked surprised. "I had no idea about that. Has his mother agreed?"

"No, but she might," insisted Neil. "She said they'd talk about it."

Mr. Hamley smiled kindly. "If I know Mrs. Sparrow, I'm afraid he won't have much success. I don't think she'd let him have anything that grows to Dotty's size or has her energy, to say nothing of her gift for making chaos."

A soft growl came from somewhere in the pen. They looked around the door in time to see Dotty take Berry gently by the scruff of the neck and lead her back to the bedding.

Neil dodged out of sight of the door.

"Dotty doesn't like them, either!" he whispered.

"Dotty's behaving badly just now, you know that," Mr. Hamley whispered back. "She could be wrong about them, and so could you. I don't have a lot of choices, Neil. Now, I don't want to keep them waiting."

Mr. Hamley turned on his heel and left Neil alone with his fears.

Neil watched the gleaming Range Rover drive away. It was fairly new and well-maintained. It looked as if it belonged to people who knew what they were doing and had their lives well organized. But that didn't make them good puppy owners.

"Dad," he said, "I didn't like the look of them. They didn't seem to care about the dogs."

"I know what you mean." Bob fingered his beard thoughtfully. "But maybe that's just their manner. They want to look businesslike. And it's up to Paul Hamley, not us."

Neil remained worried and miserable until he opened the front door to be met by Jake and Sam, falling over each other to greet him. He always felt better after a warm welcome from his dogs.

"Mom's gone back to the rescue center," said Emily, without looking up from her homework. "She's showing another candidate around. If you're going up there, say hello to Wheelie for me, will you?"

Neil was already out the door when he decided to go back for the camera. He knew that having film developed was an expensive business and that he couldn't afford to photograph *every* dog at King Street, but he'd grown attached to Wheelie.

He hurried toward the warm glow of the rescue center and headed straight for Wheelie's pen, making a big fuss over the affectionate little mongrel. Wheelie had his usual game with the rubber ball, then Neil took the camera from his pocket.

"Smile, Wheelie!" he said.

But Wheelie was already sitting up straight, as if he'd been ordered to. His ears lifted. As soon as the shutter clicked, he padded up to Neil, sniffing hopefully at the pocket where the dog treats were usually kept.

"Good dog!" Neil scratched him under his chin, where his collar should have been, and gave him a biscuit. "You know all about cameras, don't you? Someone must have taken a lot of pictures of you. They must be missing you."

He put the precious camera carefully in its case and into his pocket. Wheelie brought the rubber ball and was clearly hoping to play again, but there were other dogs Neil wanted to say hello to. He gave Wheelie one last pat.

"They must be searching everywhere for you," he said. "They're sure to find you."

He had looked in on two or three other dogs when he saw Carole leaving the office and walking toward him. There was a small woman with her who was as slender as a dancer. She had a bright, lively face. As Carole moved out of the way, Neil saw Sarah. She was holding the woman's hand and gazing lovingly up at her. Whoever she was, she'd made a big impression on his little sister.

"Hi, Neil!" called Carole. "Come and meet Bev. Bev, this is Neil, my son."

Bev smiled broadly. The dog hair on her clothes showed that she had already come into contact with the occupants of the kennel blocks. Inside the rescue center, a dog in the nearest pen trotted to the mesh to see what was going on and Bev knelt down and held out her hands toward him, looking carefully at his eyes.

"Looks like cataracts to me," she remarked.

"Yes, advanced cataracts," said Carole. "But he's old, and they don't bother him, so Mike doesn't want to operate. You should see the Afghan in the next pen. She's a beauty."

"Oh, yes!" said Bev, moving on to admire the sleek and graceful Afghan hound. "Isn't she wonderful? I think people buy these dogs because they look so stylish, then they find out how much grooming they need. Afghans can be a little temperamental, too, can't they?"

"Never look them in the eye," said Bob as he arrived to join them. "You're right. This one was brought to us by an owner who just couldn't cope with all the grooming and walking. If you come to work here, grooming Natasha may well be one of your first jobs."

"Have you got dogs?" asked Neil.

Bev's face lit up. "Oh, I've never been without a dog in the house. The one we've got now, Milly, was a rescue dog from here."

Neil remembered Milly from a couple of years back, but he didn't remember Bev.

"Black-and-tan mongrel," Bev continued. "Most intelligent dog I've ever had. Which is your favorite, Sarah?"

"Wheelie," said Sarah at once. Then she thought again. "Or Scrap. Maybe Berry. I'm not sure. All of them!"

When the Parkers were all in the house and Bev had gone, Carole flopped wearily into an armchair and looked up at Bob.

"I think she's the one," she said.

"She's pretty good, isn't she?" agreed Bob. "She looks a bit thin, but I think she's tough."

"She's worked as a nurse, so she must be," said Carole. "And she's obviously a very caring person."

"She seems to know a lot about dogs," added Neil. "She looks like she feels at home with them."

"She's nice," said Sarah. "I told her all about Fudge, and she said she used to have a hamster called Twitch. And all the dogs liked her."

"Yes, they did," said Carole. "She said she's always

wanted to work with animals but never had the opportunity before. Now that her children are all grown up, she's free to give it a try. We talked about qualifications, and she's already done her Kennel Staff Certificate."

"It's a shame Kate wasn't here to meet her," said Bob. "Still, I expect they'll get along. She can start next week, and I'd be really happy about that. There's enough work right now to keep an army busy."

"Her references are excellent," said Carole. "She's got enough sense and initiative to see what needs to be done and do it. Yes, I think we should offer her the job."

"Good," said Neil, "I'm glad that's decided. But aren't we forgetting something?"

Everybody exchanged puzzled looks.

To Neil, the answer was obvious. "Dotty! We still haven't done anything about Dotty's puppies! If we don't find homes for them soon, Mr. Hamley might end up selling them to those Wobbly-Bell people!"

Bob scratched his beard. "Hang on a minute, Neil —"

Neil interrupted him. "I know what you said, Dad, but I wouldn't trust them with any dog. Not even a toy dog that runs on batteries!"

CHAPTER SIX

"What's all this about?" asked Carole.

Neil and Bob told her about the Waverley-Bells and their visit to view Dotty's three energetic offspring.

"Just because they didn't get down on their hands and knees to play with the puppies," said Carole, "doesn't make them heartless. They have their license to breed dogs, don't they?" Neil was about to ask her what sort of license they needed, but Sarah distracted everybody carrying on about how wonderful Bev was. Then Emily piped up with her concerns about finding Wheelie's owner.

"When you get your pictures developed, Neil," she was saying, "we could scan the best one and put it on some posters. And we could put him on the web site, too. The way he keeps hopping into cars, he could have come from anywhere in the country."

"Well, he certainly isn't local," said Neil. "I think he would have been claimed by now if he was."

"But if you left a car door open and a dog jumped in, you'd know about it, wouldn't you?" Emily went on, thinking out loud. "You couldn't just drive off without knowing he was there. Unless he got into a van of some sort, or a trailer, and got out again as soon as it stopped. He could be from anywhere, Land's End to John O'Groats, for all we know."

She kept talking about Wheelie, but Neil didn't hear any of it. He was aware of Jake and Sam under the table at his feet. Not long ago, Jake had been as small and vulnerable as Dotty's puppies. He wouldn't have wanted anyone to handle him the way the Waverley-Bells had handled Beauty, Berry, and Scrap, without even a pat or a kind word. Finally, unable to shake off the worry, he slipped out to the boarding kennels.

"No, Dotty, you're not going anywhere," he said, patting the large Dalmatian as she leaped to greet him. "I just need to think."

He knelt on the floor, and Scrap settled down in his lap. He kept one arm across Dotty's warm, smooth back and stroked Beauty's head with his free hand. The gentle, repeated stroking of her soft fur helped him concentrate.

Carole had said something about breeding kennels needing a license. He knew there was a law about that. He just couldn't remember what it was. It might be worth finding out, though.

"Down you go, Scrap," he said, gently lifting the sleepy pup from his lap. "I'll see you all in the morning."

He found Bob in the office, studying a spreadsheet on the computer.

"Dad?"

Bob swung around in the office chair. "You're still worrying about those puppies, aren't you, Neil?"

Neil nodded gloomily, and Bob went on, "Do you really think you'll be happy, Neil, whoever takes them?

I'm glad you care so much, but I do wonder if you're getting too attached to them."

"It's not like that, Dad. I just want them to be happy. But I really came to ask you about licenses."

"Oh, yes, for a breeding kennel. If they have more than two breeding females, they have to apply for a license. One of the conditions of having and keeping a license is that they have to be inspected by the local authority."

"So if they don't have a license, they're breaking the law?"

"Yes, but who says they don't? They seem pretty organized to me. I suppose it might be worth mentioning to Terri, in case she wants to check them out." Terri McCall was the local SPCA inspector. She and the Parker family had often helped each other out in the past.

"Can I check the web site, Dad?" asked Neil. "Just in case anyone's asking about the puppies?"

"Yes, I've finished here, anyway," Bob replied, closing down his program files, then standing up and shuffling his paperwork together.

Neil sat down at the computer, logged on to the Internet, and clicked into the King Street Kennels' e-mail system. Fairly quickly his face erupted in a wide grin. "Dad, there's someone out there who wants the puppies! There's a name and a phone number and an e-mail address! Quick, let's get right back to them!"

"Slow down," said Bob. "Give me the details."

Neil hurriedly scrawled the name and numbers on the back of an envelope and thrust them toward his dad.

"Copper . . . what does that squiggle say?" Bob asked as he tried to read what Neil had written. He looked more closely. "It isn't Copperthwaite, is it?" Then a broad grin spread across *his* face, too, and he chuckled. "Not Jeremy Copperthwaite?"

"Yes, that's it," said Neil. "Jeremy and Sally Copperthwaite, it says."

"Carole," called Bob, running outside.

Neil followed him into the house.

"Carole, come and see this!" Bob called up the stairs. "Jeremy Copperthwaite's got his eye on Dotty's pups!"

"Not *the* Jeremy Copperthwaite?" asked Carole, who had been putting Sarah to bed.

"How many Jeremy Copperthwaites can there be?" asked Neil.

Bob couldn't stop smiling. "Well, if Jeremy wants them, we don't need to look for anyone else." He grinned at Neil. "I went to college with Jeremy. He's from the West Country, but he married a girl from Derbyshire. The last thing I heard about them, they were settling down there, with a boarding kennel and training classes. He's probably the best dog handler I ever knew. But he didn't have Dalmatians then."

"Well, it sounds like he wants to now," said Carole. "And they couldn't go to anyone better. We'll give him a call."

There was only an answering machine at the number Bob phoned. He left a message on it, and Neil sent an e-mail.

"It'll be good to see Jeremy and Sally again," said Bob. "I'll tell Paul Hamley that I can personally recommend them."

"Do you suppose the Copperthwaites will want all of them, Dad?" asked Neil.

Carole laughed. "If Toby wants one, he can always ask Paul to keep one for him," she said. "As long as he and his mom make up their minds quickly."

Things are moving fast, thought Neil. A couple of days ago, the Hamleys seemed to think they'd never find homes for the puppies. Now, there was a choice of offers. He thought he'd better phone Toby.

There was only an answering machine at the Sparrows' number, so Neil left a message. "Hi, Toby, it's Neil," he said. "If you do want a puppy, you'd better move fast. See you tomorrow."

Hoping he wouldn't get another answering machine, he decided to phone Terri, too. He was relieved to hear her kind, reassuring voice when she answered the phone.

"Neil! Good to hear from you. What can I do for you?"

Terri listened while Neil explained about the puppies and the Waverley-Bells. When he had finished, she said, "So there's no actual cruelty going on, as far as you know?"

"Well, no."

"No neglect? Nothing likely to cause harm?"

"Nothing like that — at least, nothing I know about."

"And you haven't seen their kennels?"

"No, but Mr. Hamley says they're very good. It's just the way they are with the puppies. I know it sounds as if I'm phoning you for nothing, but . . ."

"If in doubt, Neil, always phone me," she said firmly. "Now, the name Waverley-Bell means nothing to me, but I'll make some inquiries and see if any of my SPCA colleagues know anything about them. And I'll find out if they have a license. How are Jake and Sam doing?"

"They're fine. That reminds me, I think it's time I let Jake into the yard. Bye, Terri, and thanks. Call me soon."

He found Jake sitting hopefully at the back door, so he let the dog out and stood waiting in the doorway. Jake sniffed around, chose a bush, watered it thoroughly, and scampered back in again.

"Good dog," said Neil, giving Jake a pat and ruffling his ears. He couldn't imagine life without a dog. He thought of Toby Sparrow, who wanted one so much.

"There has to be a puppy for Toby this time," he said to Emily when he found her reading in the living room. "He really wants one, and he'd be a good owner."

"Wouldn't he like a rescue dog?" said Emily.

"I think he's set his heart on a certain Dalmatian puppy," said Neil. "He's aiming for the best."

"I'm more worried about Wheelie," said Emily. "Do you think we should make some posters? We'd need thousands. And even so, we couldn't cover the whole country. I just hate to think that we might never get him back together with his owner. It would be terrible for both of them."

"Keep looking, Em," said Neil. "You'll solve it."

Neil struggled to wake up the next morning. Through a deep sleep, he heard car doors banging and a dog barking. He drifted into a dream in which Wheelie jumped into the Waverley-Bells' Range Rover and drove it away with Dotty and the puppies in the back. But there were voices outside, and the feeling that something important was happening finally pulled him out of sleep. It was unusual to hear this amount of activity so early in the day. Struggling awake, he pulled on his clothes and ran downstairs.

Sarah sat at the kitchen table, sticky with marmalade. "Morning, Neil!"

"Hiya, Squirt," Neil managed. He fidgeted and

looked around nervously. "Have I missed anything?" he asked.

Sarah giggled. "No! Only your principal."

Neil was surprised. "What? Mr. Hamley was here? What did he want?" But he didn't wait for Sarah's answer — even if she knew. Suddenly *he* knew exactly why Mr. Hamley had visited them so early.

He lunged for the kitchen door and ran all the way to the boarding kennels.

His heart was pounding.

Surely it couldn't be true.

Neil scrambled through the door of Kennel Block One, barged past his dad — who he nearly knocked over — and hurried to the end pen.

It was empty.

Dotty and her puppies were gone.

CHAPTER SEVEN

A tuft of white fur lay on the floor of Dotty's pen. Neil picked it up, wondering which one of the puppies had shed it. As he did, he realized that Bob was behind him.

"Mr. Hamley came early this morning," he said. "He's sold the puppies already, to the Waverley-Bells. I'm sorry, Neil, but it's out of our hands. They're not our dogs."

The worst thing about working with dogs was parting with them. Neil had often done so before, but he still hadn't gotten used to it. This time, he found himself empty and aching, knowing that he'd never see Beauty, Berry, and Scrap again. He wouldn't even have the satisfaction of seeing them go to kind, understanding owners who could make them happy. And how was Toby going to feel?

For once, Neil was speechless. He just nodded to his father and left for school soon after breakfast. He wasn't very hungry.

Arriving at school that morning, Neil felt that nothing could be worse. But it could. Toby Sparrow ran to meet him, his eyes shining, his voice gabbling with excitement.

"I can have a puppy! Mom says I can have one of —"

"Toby," said Neil with a heavy heart. He couldn't bear to let him go on. Toby saw the misery on his face, and his smile vanished.

"What's the matter? Is it the puppies? Are they all right?"

"I'm really sorry, Toby," said Neil. He felt rotten. "Mr. Hamley already sold them." He glanced away as Toby struggled to control his shaking lower lip.

"It's not your fault, Neil," he muttered. Then he rubbed his sleeve across his face and ran. Neil would have followed him, but, at that moment, the bell rang.

"Neil?" Mrs. Sharpe called his name as he and Hasheem walked into the classroom. "Neil, are you all right?"

Neil was still upset and angry, but he hadn't meant to let it show. "Yes, Mrs. Sharpe," he said. She looked at him for a moment, and he knew she didn't believe him.

"Well," she said, brushing something off her neat red suit, "Mr. Hamley would like to see you at morning break."

Neil didn't want to see Mr. Hamley. Maybe he shouldn't blame him for selling the pups to the Waverley-Bells. Poor Mr. Hamley couldn't have a normal family life again until the puppies were gone. And now they were. Forever.

At break, he made his way to the office.

"Neil," said Mr. Hamley. His voice was unusually gentle. "Sit down."

As he sat, Neil thought about what it must be like at Mr. Hamley's house now. Dotty must be all alone, and Neil couldn't imagine going back there. It would be too quiet with no yapping puppies, no Beauty and Berry playing hide-and-seek, no Scrap to trip over. He could picture the kitchen, with the pen dismantled and the bedding washed and neatly folded away. He thought of the day he had watched Dotty give birth to those puppies. He missed them terribly already. Especially Scrap.

"I'm sorry about the puppies," said Mr. Hamley. "I know you must be upset."

"If you'd just waited a little longer, we had other buyers lined up for them," said Neil. "One of dad's friends. And Toby."

"Yes, Neil, but I didn't know that when I made my

decision. You didn't know it, either, did you? And I really didn't think Mrs. Sparrow would let Toby have one."

"You could have asked them to wait," said Neil. He couldn't help it. "You could have talked to my dad."

"I was desperate, Neil, and the Waverley-Bells were prepared to pay at once and take them right home. They offered me less than I'd asked, because of the markings and because Scrap is so small, but what could I do? I really didn't care about the money. Rachel had been pushed out of her own home."

Neil nodded. "Is that all?" All of a sudden, he was desperate for some fresh air.

"Yes — but, Neil, don't worry about the Waverley-Bells. I know you didn't like them, but they seem to know what they're doing. I'm sure they're all right."

There was no point in arguing. Neil went out to the playground. He saw Chris and Hasheem talking to Toby Sparrow and Emily. Chris was giving Toby a friendly pat on the shoulder, and Hasheem was offering him some candy. As Neil joined them he saw that Toby looked pale and was still a little pink around the eyes.

"I wish you could have had one of them, Toby," said Neil. "I did what I could."

Toby nodded bravely. "Mom might let me have a rescue dog, anyway," he said. But Neil knew he had set his heart on a Dalmatian puppy. When the bell rang, they headed for their classrooms.

"I suppose he'll get over it," said Hasheem. "What are they like, those Wobbly-Bells or whatever they're called? They sound so snooty, with a name like that."

"Their Range Rover's a lot nicer than ours," said Neil. "Newest model, latest registration."

"Really?" said Chris. "I've seen one like that. It goes past our place a lot. I noticed it because it always has dog stuff in it."

"Are you sure?" asked Neil.

"Positive. I'm sure I've even seen some dogs being carried around, too. It only showed up lately. It's usually parked on Riverside Road, outside the big red-brick house. That's not far from Toby's place, is it?"

"It might be worth a look," said Neil before he and Emily went to their different classrooms. "What do you think, Emily?"

"Hurry up, Neil!" whispered Hasheem. "We don't dare be late for anything these days! Sharpe's the word!"

Neil and Emily didn't usually sit together at lunchtime, but today they somehow ended up at the same table. Mrs. Sharpe, carrying a plate of quiche and salad, came to join them.

"Is there room for one more?" she said, smiling. She always sat with the pupils, never with the teachers.

"There's a seat here, Mrs. Sharpe," said Emily, and moved her plate over a little.

Neil looked around the room to see who was looking at them. Sitting with a teacher was seriously uncool.

However, when Mrs. Sharpe began to talk, he found her really surprising. She was as strict as a sergeant major in class — nobody dared step out of line — but she was friendly and good-natured, too, especially out of class.

"What sort of dog do you have, Mrs. Sharpe?" asked Emily.

Mrs. Sharpe laughed. "You two live and breathe dogs! I don't have one. Not everyone does!"

"There's dog hair on your sleeve," Emily pointed out. "I just thought . . ."

"Oh, that!" Mrs. Sharpe turned her arm so she could see and picked a few stray hairs from her suit.

"It's a complete mystery. Ever since I moved in, I've been finding dog hair — mostly on the furniture, but they seem to end up on my clothes, too. I don't understand it."

Emily carefully picked a hair or two from the red sleeve. She inspected them closely and held them up to the light.

"What's so interesting?" asked Neil.

"Probably nothing," said Emily innocently, and went on eating her lunch.

After school, Neil and Emily rode their bikes up to Riverside Road. There was no sign of the Range Rover, but they found the house Chris had talked about. It was tall and spacious, with a neatly tended front yard and elegantly draped curtains at the windows. A gravel path led down one side of the house to the yard and buildings behind it.

"Neil! What if somebody comes?" said Emily.

Even as she spoke, a car drew up. Neil stopped, but, to his relief it wasn't the new Range Rover. The car being parked outside the house was a red Metro, and a young woman in a tight dark suit stepped out. She smiled at Emily.

"Aren't they here yet?" she said. Her manner was bright and easygoing. "They told me to come at four. This is the right house, isn't it? The Waverley-Bells?"

"Yes," said Emily. "But I don't know . . ."

"Are you getting a puppy, too?" She smiled brightly.

"I saw their ad in the paper. They've got Chihuahuas, and I think they're so sweet! So they said to come here at four o'clock, and they'd have one ready for me."

"As simply as that?" said Neil. "Didn't they want to know anything about you?"

The woman laughed. "Why should they need to know anything about me?" She glanced at her watch. "I was afraid I'd be late. I've just been to the library to get a book about dogs. I thought I'd better find out something about looking after them."

"Shouldn't you have done that sooner?" demanded Neil, but she only gave an awkward little laugh.

"My friend got a puppy from here," she said. "They're really good. She said the kennels were lovely — nice and clean and roomy. What sort of puppy are you getting?"

"We're not buying a puppy today," said Emily. "It's time we went, Neil. We can't do anything more here right now."

"Oh, did you just come to have a look at the puppies?" asked the young woman.

"Yes, I guess we did," said Emily, "but we're not staying."

"Just a minute," said Neil, and he turned to the woman. "It's not a good idea to buy a dog until you really know what you're getting yourself into. They're a lot of work, even little ones, and you need to know about how to take care of them. But if you do get a puppy today, take it to Mike Turner, the vet in Compton. He'll check it over and give it its shots and advise you about it."

The woman looked quite bewildered.

"Trust us," said Emily, "we know what we're talking about. Come on, Neil!"

"So that's how they do business," Neil growled as they wheeled their bikes away. "They don't care who they sell to. Anyone who can read an ad in a newspaper can just turn up and buy a puppy. It's like a supermarket."

A small figure on the other side of the road waved at them.

"There's Toby!" said Emily, waving back.

"Not again!" said Neil. "I can't get away from him today."

"What's the matter with Toby?" demanded Emily crossly.

"Nothing. I just feel so rotten when I see him, because of the puppies." But Toby had already crossed the road to talk to them. And he looked as bright and cheerful as he had first thing that morning, when he still hoped for a Dalmatian puppy of his own.

"Neil, Em, I've had a great idea!" he announced. "It might not make a lot of sense, but you won't laugh, will you?"

"Let's hear it," said Neil.

"The people who bought Scrap," began Toby, "they bought him to breed him, didn't they? I want a puppy of my own, and I want one like Scrap. I don't mind if I have to wait, even if I have to wait for years and years. When he's old enough to breed, there'll be puppies, and maybe I can buy one of those! What do you think, Neil? Son of Scrap!"

For Toby's sake, Neil gave an encouraging nod, but he wasn't really thinking about Toby's idea. A completely new thought had occurred to him.

"It's possible, Toby," he said, "but it would be a long wait. Emily and I have to get home now. Bye!"

"Em, I just realized something," he whispered urgently as soon as Toby was out of earshot. "I should have seen it sooner."

"Surprise me."

"The Waverly-Bells want dogs to breed, right?"

"Right."

"But they said it themselves — Scrap's undersized! That's why they offered a low price for him! Who wants to breed from the runt of the litter?"

"What about breeding from Beauty and Berry, then?"

"I'm not sure. Maybe they're good breeding stock, but Scrap certainly isn't. They don't want to breed him, they want to sell him." Neil was on a roll now. "And, from what we've just seen, they couldn't care less who they sell to. I bet Mr. Hamley wouldn't be so happy knowing that Dotty's puppies could be going to irresponsible owners!"

"So?" asked Emily.

"So we need to get them back," replied Neil. "Fast!"

CHAPTER EIGHT

Neil and Emily arrived home at King Street just in time to meet Bob on his way back from walking two large, glossy black Labradors that were boarding at the kennel. Neil went with him to take them back to their pen.

"Dad," he said, "I've just found out something about the Waverley-Bells." As they filled the dogs' dishes with water, he told him about the young woman who had arrived to buy a puppy.

"They were going to sell her a puppy then and there, no questions asked," concluded Neil. "They knew nothing about her, and she knew nothing about dogs."

"Maybe." Bob thought a minute. "But maybe they'd talk to her at that first meeting and decide whether to let her have a puppy or not."

"Ha!" countered Neil grumpily.

"I agree, it's not a good way to sell dogs."

"But that's not all," said Neil. Bob locked the door and they walked down to the house. "Toby Sparrow said something that got me thinking. He was talking about how Scrap would father a litter of puppies one day, and he might be able to have one."

"He'd have a long wait!" Bob laughed.

"That's not the point. We've been missing something all this time. Scrap isn't the kind of dog you would breed, is he, Dad?"

"I see what you mean," said Bob, and tugged thoughtfully at his beard. "You could be on to something there. Scrap's a wonderful little puppy. He'd make someone a perfect pet. But he's not right for breeding."

"So why did they want him? Do you suppose they're going to sell him?"

Bob was quiet and thoughtful for a few seconds. Then he said, "I think that must be it. They've bought him for a knockdown price so they can sell at a good profit. You're right, Neil, we should . . ." Bob hesitated. "*I* should have seen that earlier."

"So they lied to Mr. Hamley," said Neil grimly.

At the front door, Jake and Sam raced to meet them. A delicious smell of cooking beckoned from the warm kitchen.

"What about Beauty and Berry?" said Neil. "Do

you suppose they'll sell them, too? They did say that their markings were poor."

"That may just have been an excuse to force the price down," said Bob. "Mike and I were just talking about this. You know about the problems with breeding dogs to meet show standards, don't you, Neil?"

"Yes, you end up breeding in bad points as well as good ones," said Neil, pleased to show that he understood. "So if a dog has a good point, like perfect markings, that can be passed on to its puppies. But it'll pass on weaknesses, too, like poor eyesight or a nervous temperament."

"Right. Dalmatians sometimes have problems with their hearing. There's been too much effort over the years to breed Dalmatians with perfect spots, and they've ended up producing dogs with poor hearing. So we now have a lot of perfectly marked Dalmatians going deaf."

"There's nothing the matter with Beauty's and Berry's hearing." Neil chuckled. "They know all about the doorbell!"

"So they could be good as breeding females," said Bob. "Anyone with sense would want a generally healthy dog, rather than a perfectly marked one. They might breed from them, or they might sell them, I can't be sure. But I'm sure about Scrap."

"We need to tell Terri," said Neil.

"What can she do?" said Bob. "They've been dishonest, but not cruel."

Even so, Neil dialed the SPCA inspector's number. She sounded out of breath when she answered the phone.

"I've just come in from one call," she gasped, "and I have to run off to another. Is it about the new kennels in Colshaw?"

"Yes. I think they —"

"Don't worry, Neil, I'm following up on it. I'll be in touch soon. I have to go now — I have a cat to rescue. Bye!"

Neil put the phone down. He wished he'd been able to explain more to Terri about the Waverly-Bells, although, as Bob had pointed out, there was no reason to think they'd been cruel to any animal. At least she was already on the case. He still felt uneasy, though.

He found Emily sprawled on the living room floor, reading the *Compton News*. Jake, who seemed to think this was some sort of game, tried fighting with the paper and, when Emily stopped him, he took a good lick at her instead.

"Behave, Jake!" she said. Giving in, she stood up and lifted the paper off the floor. "Look at this, Neil. In the ads."

Neil took the paper and read the advertisement she was pointing to. *"Puppies — Westies, Chihuahuas, retrievers, Dalmatians, ready now,"* he read aloud.

"And there's a Compton phone number, but no name. This must be the Waverley-Bells. And it sounds like a big operation. If they go on like this, Compton will be full of dogs belonging to clueless owners."

"Exactly!" said Emily.

"Well," said Neil defiantly, "I don't want Scrap to be one of them."

Neil went to bed that night still anxious about the puppies. It wasn't just Dotty's puppies anymore, but all the litters in the Waverley-Bells' kennels. He slept badly and woke while it was still dark. Knowing that he couldn't get back to sleep even if he tried, he decided he might as well get up and take the dogs out.

Quietly, he pulled on warm clothes, went down-stairs, and whistled for Sam and Jake, who were de-lighted to have an early walk. Jake galloped from one clump of grass to the next, snuffling into every corner. Sam, after an initial burst of energy, settled down to a trot at Neil's heels.

Turning up his collar against the cold, Neil won-dered how long it would be before Scrap was sold. There didn't seem to be much he could do to prevent it, but if he could just be there, at the kennels in Riverside Road, at least he'd know what was going on. Perhaps he could do something if he was on the spot.

He turned for home and saw that the light was on in Emily's room. He found her dressed and putting her shoes on.

"You going out already?" he said.

"I couldn't sleep. I thought I may as well go down to the rescue center."

"How about coming with me instead? I'm going to visit the Waverley-Bells."

"It's a little early, isn't it?"

Neil thought for a moment. "Well, by the time we've grabbed something to eat and walked up there, it won't be 'a little early,' will it? We *have* to go up there. We can't just leave things the way they are. At least if we can find out a little more about them, I can report back to Terri and give her something to work on."

"So what do we do?" demanded Emily. "Turn up on the doorstep and say, 'Hi, we're checking you out to see if we should report you to the SPCA?' We have to have some reason for being there. I wonder if we could pretend to be choosing a puppy?"

"I don't suppose even they would sell to somebody our age," said Neil. "And I was here when the Waverley-Bells came to look at the puppies. They might remember me."

"Your face isn't that unusual," said Emily. "They were looking at the puppies, not you. Let's go over there and say . . . Oh, what can we say . . . ?"

"Got it!" said Neil as inspiration struck. "Let's say we want to help with the dogs! Tell them we love animals and we heard about the kennels and we want to help. Then we can get a good look at how they do things."

"And see Dotty's puppies," said Emily.

"And get some evidence for Terri," said Neil. "Just hold on a minute, Em."

As Emily put on her jacket, Neil went to find his camera and the last roll of film. He had a feeling they might be needed.

CHAPTER NINE

Neil and Emily stood at the door of the elegant house on Riverside Road. When the door opened, Emily put on her most appealing smile.

"Hello, are you Mr. Waverley-Bell?" she asked. "This is where the new kennel has just opened, isn't it?"

"It certainly is." He smiled down at her. "Did you come to buy a puppy? You'd have to bring your parents with you, you know."

Neil gritted his teeth, but Emily kept her wide-eyed, innocent expression.

"No, we don't want to buy one," she said, "but we'd like to help with them. We're very experienced with dogs."

"We thought you might want some help with feeding and cleaning," Neil added. "Like my sister said, we're used to doing that."

Mr. Waverley-Bell looked carefully at Neil.

"Haven't I seen you before?" he said. "Weren't you at King Street Kennels the other day, when we went to look at some puppies?"

Neil was about to deny it, but he thought twice.

"Yes," he said. "We help out there, too."

"But it looks really, really good here," said Emily, quickly changing the subject. Just then, there was a call from the top of the stairs.

"Charles, have you done the nine-thirty check?" It was the loud, no-nonsense voice of Pamela Waverley-Bell as she hurried downstairs. "We've got buyers coming all morning, we have to make sure we're all spick-and-span for . . . oh! Visitors already? I'm afraid you're too early to see the dogs."

"We're here to help," said Emily quickly.

"They tell me they have experience," added Mr. Waverley-Bell, who seemed to like the idea of having help at the kennels.

"We just like helping with dogs," said Neil.

"Well, if you're not afraid of hard work, we do need all the help we can get," she said. "We might even pay you something if you're as good help as you say you are. Welcome aboard. Charles will show you the kennel block. Oh, and Charles . . ."

She lowered her voice, but Neil and Emily heard what she said to him.

"Charles, if that silly girl does come back, try and sell her a Chihuahua this time. I don't know why she was so confused yesterday. I told her she'd have to let us know for sure this morning whether she's buying or not."

Neil and Emily exchanged looks as Charles Waverley-Bell led them down the path to the back of the house. There was a clean yard, fenced on three sides, with a row of outbuildings on the fourth.

"This was a stable and storage space at one time," said Mr. Waverley-Bell, opening the door of the long, whitewashed building. "We converted it into a kennel. I think you'll be impressed."

They were. It was a well-lit building, with spacious pens against the wall. Opposite the pens, there were shelves where packages of dog food, dishes, and cleaning fluids were neatly stacked. Mops and brushes stood in a corner.

"It's almost as good as King Street!" whispered Emily.

Neil hadn't imagined anything like this from the Waverley-Bells. At least it meant that the puppies weren't suffering from bad conditions. He followed Charles Waverley-Bell as he patrolled the long row of pens.

"Two retrievers in here, twelve weeks old, one male, one female," he said, pointing to a pen as he walked past it. "Chihuahuas in here, three females, one male, ten weeks old. Westies, three, two male, one female, ten weeks. Three Dalmatians — but you know about those, don't you? In the adjoining room" — he opened a door — "three breeding females, one retriever, two Westies, all expecting litters within the next couple of weeks."

Neil was already kneeling in front of the Dalmatians' pen. The puppies ran to him with little yaps of greeting.

"Hi, Scrap!" he said. "They must remember me — from that day at King Street," he added quickly. "Hello, Beauty. Hello, Berry, you little rascals!"

"Don't fuss over them," ordered Mr. Waverley-Bell. "It's not good to get too fond of the dogs. This is a commercial kennel, run to make a profit. The dogs are here to be sold or bred. Mostly, we don't even use their names."

Emily was on her knees in front of the Chihuahuas.

"They're no bigger than frogs!" she said. "They're gorgeous! Look, Neil, they're so sweet!"

Neil tried to agree that they were "sweet," but couldn't quite manage the word. "They're nice dogs," he said.

"That's right, but don't get sentimental about them," said Mr. Waverley-Bell. He walked past the pens, without a glance at the puppies pawing and yapping at the mesh, and pointed out a chart on the wall.

"They were all fed and the pens cleaned at seven-thirty this morning," he said. "The nine-thirty check is to fill the water dishes, check all the puppies are well, and clean the pens again. We have to be very thorough on Saturdays, when we have more customers than usual. Feeding again at eleven-thirty, cleaning at two, cleaning and feeding at five and eight. Pens are cleaned one at a time, and the dogs put in the yard while the pens are being washed down."

"Don't you ever play with them?" said Emily.

Mr. Waverley-Bell frowned. "They're not toys," he said. "Get started now, before the customers arrive. Start with Pen One — that's the retrievers — and work your way along. Mark the chart on the wall when each pen has been done. And please be sure that the dogs are looking their best. Customers will arrive soon!"

With that, he returned to the house. Neil and Emily mopped and scrubbed and shook out the bedding and, knowing that the Waverley-Bells were out of the way, made a fuss over the pups. Neil took a sneaky look at a pile of papers on the office desk. There were various notes scribbled down on different pieces of paper.

"Look at this!" he said, craning his head around and reading aloud from the notes. "It says, *Dalmatian dog, too small — sell. Chihuahuas two larger females, poor bone structure — sell, don't breed.* I'll photograph that. This looks like pretty suspicious business to me."

"I suppose it's all right if they're honest with the

buyers," said Emily, "and tell them that the dogs have faults. If they try to pass them off as excellent show dogs, then it's dishonest."

Neil took the photograph and knelt on the floor beside the Westies. Their stubby tails were wagging furiously.

"They're desperate for attention," he said. Then he jumped to his feet, put a camera behind his back, and tried to look busy as Mrs. Waverley-Bell strode in.

"I've got someone arriving soon to buy a female retriever," she said and looked thoughtfully into the pen. "I'll offer the smaller one. The other one will do for breeding."

"Pamela," called her husband. "We have a visitor."

Mrs. Waverley-Bell turned sharply and strode out to the yard.

"Do you have an appointment?" she asked.

"No," replied a woman's voice, "but I would very much like to see you."

"That's Toby's mom!" whispered Emily.

"Stay out of sight," Neil whispered back. "I want to see what happens." They stood to one side of a window and watched as Mrs. Sparrow told the Waverley-Bells why she was there.

"My son had his heart set on a Dalmatian puppy," she explained. "I intended to buy it for him, but I learned too late that you'd bought it to breed. My son wanted him so much, I wonder if you'd consider selling him?"

"That's a mistake," whispered Neil. "If they know she really wants him, they'll push the price up."

"A Dalmatian pup," said Mrs. Waverley-Bell thoughtfully. "Yes, I know the one you mean. I'm afraid, Mrs. . . . er . . ."

"Sparrow," she said.

". . . I'm afraid, Mrs. Sparrow, you put me in a difficult position. The dog is a valuable stud dog. We're very eager to breed him. He has an excellent pedigree and some fine qualities."

"What a whopping lie!" whispered Emily.

"A good pedigree? Oh. I didn't think he was that valuable. I know a little about dogs myself, I —"

"No, he's worth a lot of money," interrupted Mr. Waverley-Bell.

"But you do have two females with the same pedigree, too?" asked Mrs. Sparrow.

"Oh, but what we really needed was a stud dog," Mrs. Waverley-Bell said firmly. "I wish I could help you. I'd hate to think of your son being disappointed, but we have a business to run."

"I can't believe this!" muttered Neil.

"What a shame, though," went on Mrs. Waverley-Bell, "about your little boy. I wonder, Charles, could we let the Dalmatian go?"

"We have to consider what we paid for him," he said, "and the cost of buying another dog as good as this one."

"Yes, I understand that," said Mrs. Sparrow.

"I suppose," he went on, "we could just about afford to let him go for — what do you think, Pamela? — for three hundred and fifty."

"What!" whispered Neil.

"I'm sorry," went on Mr. Waverley-Bell, "but he's really worth more."

"That's not what they told Mr. Hamley," whispered Neil to Emily. "He said they gave him a low price because Scrap was a runt."

"Excuse me, I think there's someone at the door," said Mr. Waverley-Bell. He gave a charming smile. "It may be the young lady who wanted a Chihuahua." And he left his wife with Mrs. Sparrow.

"I'm sorry," said Mrs. Sparrow. "Three hundred and fifty is impossible."

"I wonder." Mrs. Waverley-Bell seemed to be hesitating. "Perhaps we could go down to three hundred and twenty. I'd have to ask Charles."

"This can't go on!" Neil muttered fiercely. "She's trying to force Mrs. Sparrow to pay too much for him — just for greed! And I'm not going to stay here and watch a rip-off!" He marched out into the yard.

"Hello, Mrs. Sparrow!"

"Neil Parker!" she exclaimed.

"Have you two met?" demanded Mrs. Waverley-Bell. She looked quickly from one to the other with suspicion in her eyes. "Is something going on here? What's that in your hand?"

Neil had forgotten that he was still holding his camera. He took a step away from her.

"You can't come in here and take photographs! Hand that over!"

"It's my camera!" protested Neil, but she grabbed for it, anyway.

There was a cry of "Leave him alone!" from Mrs. Sparrow, and "Stop it!" from Emily as Neil backed away and Mrs. Waverley-Bell reached for the camera. From somewhere on the path, there was a call of "Pamela!" Turning at the sound of her name, she lost her footing, stumbled heavily, and grabbed at Neil.

Neil was knocked off balance. There was a crash and a splintering of glass.

Mrs. Waverley-Bell struggled to her feet. Neil stood looking at the broken camera on the ground, not quite able to believe what had just happened. For the moment, he was too stunned to be angry.

Then, walking purposefully down the sidewalk, wearing her SPCA uniform, came Terri.

CHAPTER TEN

"**T**his lady," said Charles Waverley-Bell, "is Terri McCall, from the SPCA." He was still smiling warmly, but Neil could see the anxiety in his eyes. He gave a puzzled look to the broken camera on the ground but was more concerned with Terri.

Mrs. Waverley-Bell ignored the camera and the bewildered Mrs. Sparrow. She extended a hand to Terri.

"Very nice to meet you," she said. "I'm sure you'll find everything here in order."

"It certainly looks very efficient," said Terri, glancing through the open door at the pens and the puppies. "May I see your license, please?"

"Where is our license, Charles?" asked Mrs. Waverley-Bell after the tiniest pause. "I think it's in the desk, isn't it? I know it should be on the bulletin board, but we've just opened here." Neil could see she was desperately playing for time.

"Don't you remember, dear, we had to return it?" said her husband. "They made a mistake with . . . er . . . the address, so we sent it back and asked for a replacement."

Terri stopped smiling. "Perhaps I should come to the point," she said. "No application has been received. You haven't applied for a license to breed dogs. I've checked with the Village Council."

"It must have been lost in the mail," suggested Mr. Waverley-Bell, still trying to rescue the situation.

"You do realize," said Terri, being firm but very polite, "that it's illegal to set up a breeding kennel without a valid license."

The Waverley-Bells looked at each other. Mr. Waverley-Bell tried a different tactic. "Yes, but that's not really something that concerns you as an SPCA inspector, is it? I mean, what you really came about, my dear, is the welfare of the dogs, and you can see that they are extremely well cared for here. We can dispense with all this silly license business, can't we? I'm sure you have more important things to do than chase around after licenses."

Terri held her ground. "I have to uphold the law," she said. "You are breeding animals without a license. As you did when you were based in Kent, using the name Pamela Bell, when the officials there ordered you to close down your kennel."

In spite of the disaster with his camera, Neil felt a smile tugging at the corners of his mouth. Terri had done her homework.

Pamela Waverley-Bell was growing red in the face.

"That's just typical," she snapped. "All we want to do is run a business. We're efficient, we're well organized, and we work extremely hard. And you want to deprive us of our livelihood for a silly detail like a license. We're getting one, of course. We've just been too busy doing more important things, like looking after our dogs. We're trying to make a living, and what's the matter with that?"

"You don't care about your dogs," said Neil, and everyone turned to look at him. "That's what's the matter. You think the most important thing in all this is the money you make. You only take care of the dogs because you want them to get a good price. You don't care about them as dogs. Real, live dogs, with feelings."

"Well said, Neil!" said Mrs. Sparrow.

"I must ask you both to cooperate," said Terri to the Waverley-Bells. "You are not really at an advantage here. This is the second time you have failed to purchase a license for a business of this nature."

"Is there anybody around?" called a voice. Neil and Emily recognized it at once. So did the three little Dalmatians, who started a chorus of excited yaps and cries.

"Over here, Mr. Hamley!" called Emily.

Mr. Hamley strode down the path, his face set and grim. Neil knew that look. It meant someone was in big trouble.

"This is ridiculous!" complained Mrs. Waverley-Bell. "It's like Main Street here today!"

"Good morning, Terri," he said briskly. "Neil, Emily, I might have known you'd turn up. Mrs. Sparrow, good morning! Now, I'll come straight to the point." He turned to face Mr. Waverley-Bell. "I've brought back your check. I wish to withdraw from the sale, and I want the puppies returned to me at once."

"I'm afraid that isn't possible, Mr. Hamley," he said. "The deal has gone through. I'm not prepared to go back on it. Those dogs belong to us now."

"You won't be allowed to keep them, Mr. Waverley-Bell," Terri pointed out. "It would be better for you to return them now. At least that way you'll get back the money you paid for them."

Neil was impressed. Terri had known the question of money would bring the Waverley-Bells to their senses.

"It's not at all businesslike." Pamela Waverley-Bell sighed. "But I suppose it will have to do."

"Neil, I'm sorry," said Mr. Hamley. "You know, I was already having second thoughts about the puppies before Terri phoned me to ask me about the details of the sale. I wish I'd listened to you in the first place."

He took a check from his wallet and pushed it into Mr. Waverley-Bell's hand. "Would you bring the puppies, please, Neil?" he said. As Neil and Emily ran to the pen, neither of the Waverley-Bells made any attempt to stop them.

"Come, on then, you rascals," said Neil as the puppies jumped and clambered around him, their tails wagging and their tongues licking eagerly. "Let's get you out of here." He handed Scrap to Emily and carried Beauty and Berry out himself, one under each arm. "Are you taking them back to King Street, Mr. Hamley?"

"I'd like to, if you still have room for them," he said. "Rachel's just moved back in, and I don't want her to move out again."

"Excuse me, Mr. Hamley," said Mrs. Sparrow. "Is Scrap still for sale? Mr. and Mrs. Waverley-Bell were asking three hundred and fifty, which I thought was —"

"They asked *how* much?" Mr. Hamley gasped.

"We have to make a profit," snapped Mrs. Waverley-Bell.

"That's a great deal more than they paid me for all three of them together," said Mr. Hamley, in a voice that was frighteningly quiet. "Charles, Pamela — you are simply the most dishonest people I have ever done business with. Neil and Emily, would you take the puppies back to the car, please?"

"Just a minute," said Neil. He handed Beauty to

Emily and bent to pick up what was left of his camera. "Somebody will have to sweep up there, otherwise a puppy might get cut by broken glass."

"Neil!" exclaimed Mr. Hamley. "That's not your new camera, is it?"

"It was." Neil shrugged. "There was an . . . accident. Don't worry, though," added Neil, biting back his disappointment. "The puppies are all right, and I've still got my film with the pictures of Sam and Jake. Those are the really important things." And he smiled down into Berry's face.

"I want to have a word with these people before I go," said Mr. Hamley. "But I'll unlock the car first, and you two can hop in."

"Oh! That reminds me," said Emily as they went with him to the car. "Dogs hopping into cars! I'd almost forgotten about Wheelie!"

"What about Wheelie?" asked Neil as they settled themselves in the car with the dogs on their laps.

"I think I know who he belongs to! Remember, Mrs. Sharpe told you that her old next-door neighbor from Jedburgh had lost her dog? And Mrs. Sharpe had dog hair on her suit. She said they were on her furniture, and she couldn't understand how they got there. I think Wheelie must have arrived in Compton in a delivery van. Mrs. Sharpe's delivery van!"

"So Wheelie gets out, has a lift in the van — probably falls asleep on Mrs. Sharpe's couch — and jumps out when they get here! Nice one!"

"I checked it out," she said. "I kept some of those hairs from her suit and compared them with Wheelie's. They're a perfect match. The only thing I don't have is a description of the missing dog from Jedburgh. If Mr. Hamley can give me Mrs. Sharpe's phone number, I can call and ask her what he looked like."

"You're going to make someone very happy," said Neil, grinning.

The following afternoon, everything was busier than usual at King Street Kennels. Neil, arriving home from walking Jake and Sam, found Mrs. Sharpe just arriving and Mrs. Sparrow's car already parked in the driveway. And there was another car, one Neil couldn't remember seeing before. He could see his parents outside of Kennel Block One, talking nonstop to two visitors.

"I'll take you to meet Mom and Dad," said Neil to Mrs. Sharpe. "I don't know who that is with them."

He was able to guess pretty soon, though. There was a big, blond man and a woman with a kind face. She held Beauty and Berry in her arms.

"Hi, Neil!" called Bob. "Come and meet Jeremy and Sally. They're taking Beauty and Berry."

"Lovely puppies, aren't they?" called Jeremy Copperthwaite. "A pair of rascals — just the way we like them!"

"Great!" said Neil. "But what about Toby?"

"Look in there," said Bob, and nodded toward the door.

Jeremy chuckled and murmured something about "a sight worth seeing."

Neil went inside. In a corner, curled up on the floor, was Toby, with a tail-wagging, face-licking, little Scrap in his arms. With shining eyes, Toby looked up at Neil. "He's mine," he whispered, as if he couldn't quite believe it yet. "Really mine." He looked down adoringly at Scrap, who stretched up and licked his nose. "He's awesome. He's my best friend."

Neil nodded. He knew what that felt like.

Bob appeared at his side. "It's a good thing you discovered what you did about the Waverley-Bells when you did or this might not have happened."

Neil smiled. "They won't be able to buy and sell dogs anymore now, will they?"

"It's unlikely. This latest offense won't have done them any good at all. This business is better off without them."

"You can say that again." Neil didn't want to take himself away from the sight of Toby and Scrap, but he knew that Mrs. Sharpe would still be waiting to see Wheelie. Back outside, though, he found Carole already escorting Mrs. Sharpe to the rescue center and ran to catch up with them. He thought it would be worth seeing what happened next.

Above the barking of the rescue dogs there was a cry of joy from Mrs. Sharpe. "Wiz! It really is you! Barbara will be so glad!"

"He's called Wiz?" Neil asked. "'Wheelie' wasn't too far off the mark, then!"

Carole, smiling, opened the pen, and Wheelie immediately brought his favorite rubber ball to play with. Mrs. Sharpe played fetch with him as she talked.

"When Emily called to say you had a dog that might be the missing one from Jedburgh, I phoned Barbara, my neighbor, to let her know. She said it was the most terrible day when he disappeared. She'd taken his collar off for a bath, then someone came to the door. Then the phone rang and somebody must have left the gate open. The next thing she knew, she couldn't find him anywhere. She had ads for him all over the county, but she never thought of looking this far. She said to pass on her thanks to you for taking such good care of him."

"He's been a model visitor," said Carole, grinning, as Emily arrived to join them. "Emily was the one who figured out where he came from."

"If you can keep him here until Friday," said Mrs. Sharpe, "I'm going back to Jedburgh for the weekend and I'll take him home. Barbara says she'll be sending a check to the rescue center and that she's going to have him fitted with a microchip."

"If he's going to keep hitching rides, it might be a good idea!" said Carole.

"It's his only bad habit," said Emily. "He's very well-behaved. A lot better than these Dalmatian puppies!"

Neil walked away, meaning to join Toby and Scrap. For Toby, there was nothing in the world better than a Dalmatian puppy.

As he left the rescue center, though, he saw someone else arriving. Bob was already on his way to meet the new visitors.

"I should build a multistoried parking lot," he was saying. "Oh, it's the Hamleys! And they've brought Martin." He waved in greeting. "Hi, Paul, Rachel. Would you like to come in the house?"

"I blame myself for all this," said Rachel. She seated herself at the kitchen table with the baby in her lap. Sarah ran to put her finger in Martin's hand, and he chuckled at her. "If I hadn't walked out like that, Paul wouldn't have been so desperate to sell the puppies."

"It's not your fault," said Mr. Hamley. "Things were just completely out of control, and you'd had all you could take. Do you know, Neil, when I told her what had happened, she chewed my ear off and said she hadn't intended me to sell them to just anyone like that! Can't win, can I?"

"You'll just be in time to say good-bye to the puppies if you want to," said Neil, stroking Sam's ears.

"Before we do, Neil, we've got something for you," Mr. Hamley said. Mrs. Hamley reached into her bag and brought out a gift-wrapped package.

"That's from all of us, including Dotty," she said, smiling as she handed it to him. "It's to say thank you for all your help. We know you could use one."

Neil pulled off the paper and dropped it on the floor, where Jake immediately tore it to shreds. But, for once, Neil barely noticed the young Border collie. In his hands he held a new, stylish, state-of-the-art, out-of-this-world camera, complete with film.

"Thank you," he said. "Thank you very much."

Full of thanks and almost bursting with joy, he loaded the film and knelt down. Jake looked up, a bit of wrapping paper hanging out of his mouth. Neil pointed the camera.

"Smile, Jake!" he said.

Be sure to catch the next exciting Puppy Patrol!

SUPERDOG!

The next morning at the Hoopers', breakfast was interrupted by a phone call. It was a desperate Becky asking for Neil. Calling from a pay phone on the campsite, she'd found the Hoopers' number from directory assistance. She sounded very flustered and unhappy.

"It's Twister," she blurted out. "I don't know what's the matter with him. He still seems so sleepy. He just can't be bothered with anything. We're running again at twelve, and at this rate he won't make it up to the ring!"

Neil thought hard. "Has he been sick?" he asked in a worried voice. "Are there any other very obvious symptoms? Anything you could tell a vet about?"

"Nothing very concrete." Becky sniffed. "And anyway, there won't be a vet on-site for another couple of hours. There is one thing, though," she said slowly. "I don't know whether I'm imagining it, but his eyes look a little strange. It's like he's not focusing very well. But that's not enough to go on, is it? He's just so lethargic. Oh, Neil, what do you think I should do?"

"We'll be there just after ten," said Neil. "You've still got nearly three hours before you have to run. Why don't you take Twister for a slow, gentle walk. Try to get him warmed up a little. I don't think there's anything else you *can* do. If he's coming down with something, there won't be any help for it, Becky. You'll just have to pull out of Superdog!"

"That'd be awful," she wailed.

Becky hung up, obviously upset, and Neil went back to the breakfast table, feeling he'd been no help at all to their new friend.

After the drive to the fairgrounds, Neil and Emily found Becky and Twister sitting under an awning at the side of their trailer. Neil squatted down till his face was level with Twister's. "How're you doing, old boy?" he asked. Twister halfheartedly licked Neil's hand, then pulled away, slumping down onto the grass.

Becky shook her head. "He's never like that. He's always interested in people! He's just not himself, is he?"

"You're right, Becky," said Neil. "He's not the dog we saw yesterday afternoon."

For the next hour they walked Twister up and down, playing with him and egging Jake on to join in. The younger dog pirouetted around Twister, teasing him and even making Becky laugh. Slowly, Twister seemed to be waking up, but as eleven-thirty approached he was still sluggish and lacking the energy he was shortly going to need so badly.

"It's now or never," said Becky. "We've got to go up to the ring and check in. Do you think we should go for it, anyway?" she asked her mom.

"I don't think you can do Twister any harm," her mom replied. "If he doesn't feel up to competing, he'll let you know soon enough. And then you'll just have to accept the inevitable. Let's take plenty of water with us. We mustn't let him get dehydrated in this sun."

There were already more people in the arena than on Friday. It seemed to Neil that the atmosphere was much more intense and intimidating than it had been the previous day. And who should they run into first, but Marty!

"How's your hound today?" he sneered. "Looks a little out of it to me. I don't think his chances out there are good, do you?" He jerked a thumb in the direction of the rapidly filling arena.

Becky wasn't in the mood and ignored him.

You're very talkative today, Marty, Neil thought. *I wonder why? And you're very quick to notice Twister's below par.*

The arena was now laid out as the most complicated test of canine agility Neil had ever seen. There was still a set of weaving poles and some jumps, including a tire jump that looked frighteningly difficult. To these, a whole series of beautifully designed obstacles had been added. There was an A-frame with a peak more than two yards high; a seesaw with a board that seemed too narrow for a dog of Twister's large frame; a crossover table where the competitor had to move on command to the left or right; a couple of dog walks high off the ground, and a pause box, where Twister would have to lie down for ten seconds before tackling the rest of the course.

In the bright sunshine, Becky looked pale and nervous. Neil and Emily wished her and Angela Aslett good luck, reminded Twister he was a champion in the making, and took Jake up into the stands to wait for Twister's turn.